The House in Milan

The House in Milan

Giovanni Testori

Translated by Sidney Alexander

A HELEN AND KURT WOLFF BOOK

New York
HARCOURT, BRACE & WORLD, INC.

139147

The House in Milan

1

When the sirens started to howl, the clouds, which until then had hung quietly on the horizon, began piling up. White, yellow, gray, rimmed here and there with black, swiftly they invaded the entire sky, casting sudden sinister shadows on houses, vegetable gardens, and the first bits of countryside.

"Storm's blowing up!" people in the street were crying, anxious to get home as swiftly as possible. "Let's go! Hurry! Storm!" Meanwhile, the wind was scattering dust and dirt, soil and paper everywhere.

Cut in half by a cloud-shadow and one of the last rays of the sun, the Housing Project also went into a state of alarm. Clattering shutters. Clothes, shirts, underwear swinging on lines. A great hubbub in the halls and along the banisters. "Come in! Hurry! Hurry! Before the world comes to an end!" Words, shouts, cries, curses. The row of poplars at the fence shook from side to side.

Then from the edge of the outskirts, where the last houses gave way to dairy farms or were swallowed up in the fields, there was heard, amidst the first grumblings of thunder, the burst of anti-hail rockets. Cannonades swiftly rising and exploding whisperingly in nothingness. One to the right and one to the left; one to the east and one to the west.

2

"Go on! Shoot!" Redenta cried, not knowing at whom, as she flung the window wide open in order to snatch from the windowsill the piece of beef that was lying there wrapped in a bit of paper. "Go ahead! Shoot your rockets, bombs, madonnas, and antichrists. Go ahead! Go ahead! So then we can all be locked up in a madhouse! That's where your progress is leading us! As if the war hadn't been enough to ruin our nerves!"

A glance, no more than that, at the lights arrowing toward the south, another glance at the gloom in which the rest of the sky was sinking as in an inferno. Then, grasping the meat, she went to the table. At that very moment, a rocket exploded over her head with more clatter than the others, and set the windows trembling.

"Go ahead! Smash everything! At least then we'll have nothing more to worry about. So it was going to rain? Not at all. They don't want it to rain. Seasons? Summer, spring, autumn? Who sees them any more? Upside down! Even they are upside down! Like people, life, everything!"

Meanwhile, outside, the few drops that the rockets had permitted to fall came down—heavy, slow, feeble.

As for those splattering, some on the sill, some on the windowpane, Redenta felt a kind of furious rancor. Now, not even the sky, not even that was able to rebel. But in that case, better the Flood, better the end of the world. Because considering the way in which it was going, where else would humanity end up if not in a mental hospital? A hospital big enough to contain the entire world. And first of all, those who governed, the people with the rockets, the flying saucers, the bombs.

A crack. A brief silence. Then another crack. As if, instead of waterdrops, flies were being crunched against the earth, flung by a hand from who knows where.

Soup to be prepared, the slice of meat to pound . . . Redenta looked at it again, lying there on the table, and once more felt that sensation of fear and disgust that meat in general, and poultry in particular, always aroused in her.

"Meat at noon and meat in the evening," she said to herself.

4

"Always meat, that bachelor of a bachelor! As if he didn't know that half the population die of heart attacks because of arteriosclerosis and high blood pressure. And him with more than two hundred!"

The bachelor was her brother, with whom she had lived up to now and was going to live with, probably, to the very end. Because the idea that Gino might take a wife at the ripe age of forty-five was something she could not conceive of. Even though, from time to time, their talks would touch on Gino's girl friend, a seamstress he had been carrying on with for four years. A seamstress for poor folk, naturally. Though she tried hard to keep up to date, copying and recopying the countless patterns in the fashion magazines she brought home—*Grazia, Foemina,* and sometimes even *Vogue.* It seemed that even the working girls, nowadays, wanted to look like Paris models.

As for meat in the evening, that was one of many of her brother's habits Redenta simply couldn't take; especially since, as far as she was concerned, she could hardly swallow it down at noon. A shadow of terror fell on her, as if by first preparing it and then putting it between her teeth, she felt somehow it was too much like human flesh. Pot roast, beef, filet. All the same. Not to mention when she had a piece of liver in her hand! That darkish color, that purplish blood, those tiny nerves! Besides, the heap of corpses began to turn her stomach from the moment she saw them piled up and dangling in the windows and on the walls of the butchershop.

Because, when you came right down to it, the day the leaders, the bosses, decided to let loose all their progress and all their humanity, what would the world be reduced to, if not to a butchershop?

Another burst of rockets zoomed into the sky, to dispel, somewhere above the Pero gardens, a clot of clouds darker and more threatening than the others.

Redenta pressed her lips between her teeth. Yes, and if she heeded advice, she should think about everything during these explosions rather than that other butchershop which was the war, everything except what she had seen, passed through, experienced in that butchershop. Everything, except the burst of fire that had wiped out her Andrea without warning or anything on the Albanian front, the twenty-third of November. Poor riddled corpse. Blood everywhere. Blood flowing down his arms, his stomach, into the snow which the rulers of the world had let fall that day, perhaps because they hadn't the time or tranquillity to turn their minds to other things! You wouldn't let it happen even to a dog! And from that day on, naturally, as far as she was concerned, the human chapter was closed and closed forever. Especially for her, for the kind of character she came into the world with!

The space of a sigh, and then: a flash, longer than the others, darted down from the clouds and splintered the windowpanes. The rooms within seemed to burst into flames. Immediately after, thunder began rolling about the sky, dying away in a chain of grumblings, there, beyond the horizon.

3

Hidden against her mother's skirt, Lisetta once again felt terror-stricken. Then she whimpered like a little wounded animal and began to tremble.

"What are you afraid of, you little fool?" her mother said, trying to get the child out from under. "Sit down there and practice your writing!"

But practicing her handwriting was the last thing Lisetta felt like doing. As soon as the storm had threatened to break, the little Borgonuovo girl had rushed from the table and taken refuge in her mother's arms, where she was now. And her notebook had remained open on the table, at the page where her pencil had traced with difficulty the first row of marks.

"Look how brave Tino is. And he's younger!"

Tino, the only boy among the many Borgonuovo children on Via Aldini, had left the house at the first warnings of storm. At the top of his voice he had called Franchino from his floor, and Enrico from the floor below. Then, racing down the stairs, he had stood guard at one of the two doorways, watching in fascination, like his friends, the struggle between earth and sky. And there he was when a second lightning flash, longer and more spectral, followed the first.

"Come down!" he cried, gripped by a heedless, excited joy. "Down!"

4

She shouldn't have thought about the Albanian front, about Andrea, about all those wounds (a machine-gun burst, they said), about all that blood, all that shooting, suffering, crying, no, she shouldn't have thought about it, not even when she happened to see films that spoke from beginning to end about war, death, and massacres. Not even when there was nothing but war, death, and massacres on television at the bar on Via Zoagli or the one at Meroni's which worked one evening out of three. And even less when, just aimlessly straying, her eye happened to fall on the photograph, whether she wanted it to or not. Not the one that Andrea had sent her from the front (that one she had ripped to pieces, weeping and cursing, a few hours after receiving the news), but the other one, taken three or four months before he was called up, showing him dressed like a free private citizen. Because she no longer wanted to see around her even the shadow of uniforms, helmets, the fasces, the big boots, and all those implements. Shrunken, the piece of meat remained before her eyes as if it were the symbol of that to which, willy-nilly, all humanity sooner or later would be reduced.

Because if she suffered from nerves as she did; if, eight hours out of twenty-four, she felt that ring around her head that she felt, a ring that sometimes not even Kalmine or Saridon could free her of; if she suffered from all that and in addition had the prospect of ending her days in some poorhouse, Baggina perhaps or somewhere else, provided it wasn't one of those kept by nuns, since nuns got on her nerves . . . Nuns got on her nerves, rockets got on her nerves, meat got on her nerves, everything got on her nerves! A need to rebel, a need to spit in everybody's face, to curse everything. Sure, but how, if she lacked the necessary strength? If she were a man, that would be another story. We all know what happens when the fiancée of someone wearing pants dies. A few tears, a spell of emptiness, and in two, three months he finds himself another bride or picks up a girl friend.

But she? She was a poor deluded soul, one of those who having fixed on the face, name, and surname of a man, that was it: it was either that one or nothing and no one forever. And since the leaders, the bosses, the ones, in short, who had torn her man out of her arms with a draft notice had not brought him back to her arms, not even to see him, dress him, put him in the box—here she was then, still tied to what her Andrea had been and what he might have been. Not to a man, therefore, but to a shadow. A shadow, furthermore, that had left her without token or memory of the fact that he had been a man. Nothing. So how could she live and keep calm like the others who either had had their man or still had him? They ended up deceived? Oh, Madonna, what did this matter, compared with the other things?

8

While everyone was saying that the anti-hail rockets had again succeeded in stopping the storm, the wind began to blow up once more, stronger and more destructive than before. Paper, leaves, bits of twigs, clouds of dust rose on every side, colliding and commingling. Once more the shutters were banging against the walls. The saplings creaked and bowed.

"These cutthroat landlords!" Signora Schieppati was saying, although she was the first to know that the house was owned not by landlords but by a syndicate, and a syndicate set up for benevolent and charitable purposes. "If it was up to them, none of these houses would still be standing!"

Thin, her eyes protruding from her head, as if her seven children had sucked her dry, first of milk and then of everything else, Signora Schieppati continued to fold and refold what time and again she ended up by ironing: underwear, shirts, jerseys, and handkerchiefs. And meanwhile, as she folded and set them aside, she uttered maledictions and curses.

6

"Well, here we go!" Redenta said as her eyes turned and fell upon the piece of meat. "Here we go again!"

And when lightning flared through the window right over the meat, she cried out as if in a burst of liberation:

"At last, blessed Madonna! At last!"

First with a spark, then with a crackling immediately swallowed up in the thunderbolt, the current snapped out, and all over the Housing Project a livid, sinister semiobscurity took the place of light. In Signora Schieppati's kitchen a smell of burning was spreading.

The woman, who had stepped back, stood motionless now, trying to see what had happened. The iron was still there, intact, to the right of the washing; but at the point where the plug was attached, a kind of pale bluish smoke was streaming out.

"There! That ends it for today!" she said. However, before returning to the table, she paused for a few moments. When at last she stirred, the first thought crossing her mind, other than her ever-present concern about Sandrino, was of Enrico.

"Where's that little devil hiding?" she thought, setting her hands again to the jerseys, handkerchiefs, and underwear.

8

Lightning, thunder. Several unexpected showers. New gusts of air. Tiny whirls of leaves. Droplets, soil, garbage.

At the doorway, Tino, Franchino, and Enrico were jumping in excitement. Every lightning-flash crackling open the dark clouds was like a viper biting at their ankles. Then, in joy, fear, and delight one boy would shout, another swear, and yet another incite the tempest to redouble its fury.

Within the yellowish whiteness of the bedcover, old Oliva stared motionlessly through the window; but it was as if he saw nothing. As a result of his long legendary illness (he had been sick for more than six years) all the tenants called him "our mummy." As with other nicknames already in circulation, or about to be, it was Redenta who had hit upon this one. Once when Luciano's mother had told her how she hadn't been able to close her eyes all night because the sick man in the next room hadn't stopped moaning for a minute, she exclaimed: "Oh, Madonna, that poor mummy! The day he decides to go won't be soon enough!" From then on, the nickname was on everybody's lips until finally it came to the Olivas' apartment and, more specifically, right up to the sick man's bed. And he had smiled about it, certain that those in the Project who were only awaiting his death rattle would have to wait patiently awhile.

Actually, it wasn't as if he didn't see anything. Despite his age, eighty-two years, his vision in fact was still good. But he felt himself so cut off from the world that very little of what was happening managed to hold his interest. Besides, even now, he always kept the rosary beads in his hands, squeezing them with the joy, half animal and half innocent, with which a baby squeezes a piece of candy.

What he was waiting for was the return of his son and grandson, who would then take him, one by the shoulders and the other by the feet, and help him change his position. During the day his only pleasure consisted of those three of four changes during each of which his muscles seemed to return to normal, as if each time they had been set to rights forever. As for cleaning him up, his daughter-in-law took care of that, since his granddaughter was too young to get involved in that kind of work. Delicate work, not so much because one had to deal with a body pricked with an endless series of punctures and aching all over with weariness and maladies, but because he was, even at his age, a man, and his granddaughter, a woman.

"How much to go until five thirty, Enrica?" he said in a tone of voice which from his appearance one would have expected to be much weaker, but which managed instead to drown out the grumble of the thunder.

"What?" the daughter-in-law replied from the kitchen.

"I said how much to go until five thirty."

"It's five thirty now," the woman said.

Five thirty was the time when the son and grandson returned from work with clocklike punctuality.

"Good, then they'll be here soon," the old man said, enjoying in advance the relief that the imminent change of position would give him. But just as he began to long for that relief even more strongly than any other evening, he recalled how this very morning, as they said good-by, his son and grandson had told him that today they would be coming home later. They had to stop by at the Circle, the Party office, to talk over what was to be done about the incident of the day before.

Remembering, the old man shouted: "Those antichrists!" then, while another thunderbolt burst over his head: "What's God waiting for to burn them all alive?"

The incident of the day before concerned some posters that the grandson, together with some other members of his party, had pasted up on the walls of the Housing Project as on other houses in the neighborhood; the next morning they were found ripped off and smeared over with mud and feces. On one of them, as if they had dipped their finger not in that mixture but in ink, they had scrawled across: "Fascists! Priests! Traitors of the working class!"

"Obviously," the daughter-in-law had commented, "since they live in shit, they also use shit to write with."

So, the alleviation he missed was transmuted in his mind

12

into the pride of knowing that his son's and grandson's tardiness was motivated by what he called the Cause. The great Cause, in fact, of his family in particular, and of all honest men and men of good will in general.

10

"All this shouting, all this quarreling—for what?" Redenta said, as if there were an unexpected telepathic connection between herself and the room upstairs; or as if the storm's renewed violence had reminded her again of the last fight that took place there, in the house, a fight that had also been a kind of storm. Once more she was near the window, watching the drenching water that the wind was pitilessly whipping, as if the entire universe were about to split asunder. And she watched it in the hope and desire of being able to discern in the downpour some drop so large, so heavy, as to be no longer rain, but hail at last, a hailstorm.

"Words, insults, swearing," she continued thinking as her face was lighted up in the glow of the lamps. "And for what? For a bit of shit on a poster! Just let things go on as they're doing," she added, shouting, "and then tell me where your posters will wind up!"

Crushed to earth or against the sticks that held up the tomato plants in the garden, some pieces of paper still could be seen, here and there, about to disintegrate completely under the lash of water and of wind.

As soon as she realized that the storm showed signs of starting again, Signora Schieppati left her apartment, stood at the staircase, and began yelling:

"Enrico! Come upstairs, Enrico! Come up! The storm's starting up again!"

Snapping off the hinge on which it had swung an infinite number of times, a shutter fell from the kitchen window of the Consonni family onto the entrance.

"Help!" the boys screamed, scattering terrified into the hall. "Help!"

"What's the matter?" Signora Schieppati cried from upstairs. "Enrico! What's the matter?"

"A piece of the house fell down!" Enrico shouted.

"What?"

Signora Ruschetti, too, had come out of her door and, leaning over the banister, was also asking excitedly what had happened.

"A piece of the house fell down!"

"A piece of the house? How come? From where?"

"Nothing to be scared about!" Tino put in. He had had the courage to return outside and see what had happened. "It was a shutter. It came loose. . . ."

Thus, while other tenants, their eyes popping, leaned over the staircase or stood in doorways, the wind continued to whirl all around the big apartment house and the rain pelted down without, however, ever quite becoming a hailstorm, as, indeed, Redenta in the kitchen was still hoping, her desire quickened by the thud of the shutter.

When these and other indications piling up soon after were about to convince her that, finally, this time her nerves would have the release they longed for, and that the hail would destroy leaves, flowers, grass, and vegetables, everything in fact that man and springtime had managed to produce by then, the anti-hail bombardment resumed on a large scale, just as if it had never taken place before.

Busy preparing vegetables, Redenta immediately felt compelled once more to take opposing sides in the battle. "That'll do it." "No, it won't." "Now it's starting again." "They're winning." "No." "Yes." "Yes." "No . . . "

From time to time she raised her eyes from the table and observed, now with exaltation, now with disappointment, the change of darkness into light, the unforeseen opening of blue gashes and their equally unforeseen closure in scurrying clouds.

These alternations went on for several minutes, until gradually the wind and rain seemed to calm down, this time for good. There was a long pause of suspension and expectation in the air, as if the opposing forces were signing an armistice. Then, little by little, the tension lessened.

"So they've cut it short today too!" Redenta muttered. "They've won again, those pigs!"

13

Old Oliva tried to stretch his legs to another position than the one he had kept them in before, but the stab of pain forced him to stop halfway. Oh, he must be patient. He simply had to wait until his son and grandson arrived. If today he should be cheated of the only meager relief life had left him, that is, the pleasure of shifting position, he knew whom to thank for it: "Those antichrists, those traitors of the Communist Party!"

With this invective, the old man's body knotted up all over. His fists tightened, and within his right hand the rosary beads crunched as if about to break. Then, suddenly he heard again in his ears, word for word, as if rising from the depths of a tomb, his son's, daughter-in-law's, and grandson's description of the great havoc; once more, his eyes saw the fragments of the poster falling, filthied with stains, obscenity, and blasphemy, like shreds of flesh dangling from a crucifix.

The Villa family, they were the black pit out of which evil crawled snakelike through the entire house. They . . . they who would have spat even on Jesus Christ had they seen him passing down the street. Yes, they were the ones, whose chief business in life was cursing, hating, thinking bloody thoughts.

Thus, as the lamps intermittently flashed on and off, indicating that the current would soon be back in the Housing Project, old Oliva began to review in his mind all the members of that scoundrelly family. First the father. Then the mother. Finally the three children. The oldest, who was the least bad, perhaps because he got all the evil out of his system in the gym. The second, Carlo, who, if he could, would burn everything: priests, bishops, nuns, churches, oratories, and perhaps the entire world that wasn't inclined to put itself under the protection of his hammer and sickle. And the girl, who hadn't become a daughter of Satan pure and simple, only because her personality and ugliness had never induced any man to come really close enough.

16

14

Her mind full of worries, and continuing to move busily between the pots and the stove, Amilcare Villa's wife also finally decided to look out the window to see what might be happening, and thus she saw the first blaze of light opening in the leaden gray of the sky.

15

Two floors below, Signora Schieppati had tried to resume her ironing when the bulbs lit up again; and then, sure now that the electric iron had burned out, she busied herself throwing back the mound of laundry into the basket. As she stopped for a moment, she was struck by the rays that were flooding into the house from outside, lending a strange festive air to the miserable squalor of her kitchen.

16

In the doorway, the children, joined finally by Remigio and Aldino, were gazing intently at all the devastation provoked by the storm. Flowers, heads of lettuce, small tomato and potato plants, rows of carrots, everything crushed, uprooted, blown away. And scraps of newspapers and posters over everything.

But although they rushed about looking everywhere, not even the shadow of a hailstone could they find. Then Tino turned toward the wreckage of the shutter and, calling on his friends to help, tried to remove it. But he soon realized it wasn't worth the effort, and looked up toward the windowsill to see what the shutter had carried with it.

"Look," he cried, "it's taken half the wall with it!"

A good third of the windowsill was smashed. On top of the jamb, a hole gaped open like a wound, much larger than those left all over the façade by aerial machine-gunning.

"The hook's gone, too," Enrico said.

"Well, then we'll have to look for it," Remigio said, searching the ground again.

"Yes, because if we find it, think of all the things we can do with it!" commented Tino, who was beginning to feel somewhat dissatisfied with that storm which had only half happened.

"I just said it to say something," Remigio muttered.

Now, new rumblings could be heard racing across the sky. Smothered, the thunder swelled over the entire horizon, then slowly died away in nothingness. Meanwhile, the light had continued to spread and a very fine drizzle had begun to fall from the clouds.

"What's happening?" Franco said. "Is it starting all over again?"

"The angels still got a little pissing to do," Tino commented, looking at the peaceful fall of droplets glinting in the last rays of sun.

So it was that the boys in the doorway and the tenants in their rooms saw slowly forming before their eyes the great arc of the rainbow.

"Look!" Oliva's daughter-in-law exclaimed, when the rainbow was completely drawn across the sky.

"What's there to look at?" muttered the mummy.

Without expectation, he turned his eyes to the window and for the nth time in his life saw the symbol of tranquillity and peace through every window. Then he endeavored to smile and to forget the Villa family, the havoc those wretches of the Communist Party had perpetrated, the shredded posters, the mud, the dirt, Satan, and the shit.

"I'll bet those people upstairs think it's Our Father in Heaven!" Redenta said, turning her furious eyes from the window to the table. "Imagine!" she added, as she put peas, potatoes, celery, and carrots into a potful of water. "If Our Father in Heaven really was interested in what's going on down here, he would have let it pour and pour until we were drenched clean of all these scabs on our backs! But instead . . ." Instead, with the clouds' progressive withdrawal, even that ultimate sprinkling had begun to die away.

Then Redenta finished stirring the pot for the nth time, went to the window and, saying in a loud voice: "A bit of air, good God! At least that!" she energetically flung the windows wide open.

A sweet smell of wet earth came up from the garden, suffusing the kitchen with its freshness.

Soon, as every other evening, she would stand at the window and, as every other evening, watch all her poor desperate fellow prisoners returning home one by one, even though today they'd be about a half hour late since they couldn't leave the shelters until they'd waited out the storm. First the Olivas, son and grandson. Then Signora Ribaldi. Then Ribaldi's son. Then the endless row of Schieppatis, the biggest family in the settlement; so numerous in fact as to make one wonder how they managed to live in the kind of rooms they had; the dampest in the entire house, without light and without air; holes rather, not rooms. Behind them, Renata, Luciano's sister, the one who worked at the factory, one of the few women in the housing settlement with whom she saw eye to eye, without so much as exchanging a word. Then Gino was due, provided he hadn't gone that evening to visit his seamstress. And last of all, after all the others, Luciano, who had no schedule, because he found work at the oddest hours; Luciano, that poor bastard, whom she found disgusting and yet couldn't help feeling sorry for.

One hand resting on the sill, the other holding her head, her eyes fixed alternately upon each of them, as if she wanted to snatch everything out of each of them: things that went well and things that went badly; joy and grief; troubles and secrets; everything, in short, that had happened during the day or was about to happen.

That evening, however, before settling down at the window as usual, Redenta returned to the stove, stirred the ladle in the pot, threw in a pinch of salt. Then, as her eyes fell on the piece of beef, which, shrunken but still dark red, stood out starkly against the whiteness of the plate, she went to the cupboard, took a soup plate, and, in a great hurry, covered it.

"Remigio!" Signora Balzani called at the same moment, appearing at the window. "Come upstairs! Come upstairs at once! You must finish your homework!"

"Easy," Grandpa Oliva implored in his cavernous voice. "Easy, please, easy."

The old man had summoned his son and grandson into the room to make them do what he had been waiting for all day. Kindly attentive as always, the two of them had approached the bed and drawn back first the quilt, then the blankets and the sheet.

As soon as the air touched that pile of bones, entirely hidden in the nightshirt except for the softish swell of his stomach, the old man had trembled partly with the cold and partly with relief, and around him spread, heavy and acrid, the odor of sweat and urine.

"That's it, that way, that's fine," the old man said.

The grandson, his knees leaning on the mattress for support, was making the old man's head comfortable on the pillows. From the other side, the son was doing the same with the legs, which stuck out of the nightshirt like sticks covered with wrinkled whitish skin.

"Want us to fix these, too?" the grandson asked. The grandfather said Yes. Then, snug in the thought of so much thoughtfulness, he added:

"To have such a family! That's worth living for. . . ."

One by one the pillows were turned over. And those that had become dampened, because they had been under his neck or head, were beaten and fluffed up again. Soon, the grandfather was able to savor his long-awaited pleasure.

"All afternoon," he explained, while his son pulled sheet and blanket over him, "all afternoon," he repeated, "I was waiting. But those antichrists," he added, the dim light remaining in his eyes flaring up now as he gazed at his son and grandson, "those antichrists . . ."

"It's not worth getting angry about, Grandpa," the grandson said. "God have pity on them. That's all one may hope for."

"Pity, pity! Pity, my foot! May they roast in hell and be quick about it!" the old man retorted. "How often must I tell you that because of your pity, these damned bastards are taking over the world! And once we have them here, too, in our house, what'll be the good of all your pity? Kindness yes, but balls no. And it seems to me that when you're dealing with those . . ."

This was certainly not the way they wanted the conversation to go. Hearing that tone of voice, son and grandson were almost afraid to begin. In fact, the decision reached at the meeting that had been held at the Circle was that it was necessary to answer their rivals' actions with firmness, yes, but in as civilized a way as possible.

"Well, what have you worked out?" the old man asked after a long, suspenseful pause. "Come on, speak up. What have you decided to do?" Son and grandson looked at each other for a moment.

"You tell him, Luigi," the son said. "You're more used to these things."

"Don't think it was easy, Grandpa," Luigi began, fingering the volutes of the holy water font over the night table with embarrassment. "Everybody had his say."

"Don Rinaldo, for example . . ." Luigi's father interrupted.

"Don Rinaldo, that coward! First of all, I would have filed

22

a complaint against them with the police. Names and surnames, the whole lot!"

"But in order to file a complaint . . ." Luigi tried to reply.

"In order to file a complaint? Just let me tell you—in order to file a complaint you need guts and for some time now, it seems to me, all the courage has been on their side."

"It's not a question of courage, Grandfather. It's a question of knowing who it really was."

"But everybody knows, everybody knows very well!"

"Yes, of course everybody knows," Luigi replied. "But what if we have to prove it? What proofs do we have? Neither I, nor he, nor you caught them in the act.

"And most important, let's not forget that our party is a party that's always called itself democratic," Luigi said, speaking again with his usual calm.

"Ah, democracy!" the old man struck back, completely forgetting what had been suggested to him by the rainbow appearing in the sky just a little while ago. Now his voice, phlegmy with catarrh, began to thicken and gasp. "Democracy, sure, but for the others! Democracy so that those pigs can make propaganda for their theories and their rottenness any way they like! But when it comes to us, oh, then it's charity, goodness, civilized behavior! Sure, I know all about that charity, goodness, and civilized behavior! Cowardice! Cowardice which one day or another they'll throw back in our faces, priests and nonpriests alike! Cowardice, and then fear on top of that! Fear to make a decision that will fix them once and for all! Yes, but you," he continued, after having got rid of the catarrh, spitting into a handkerchief which he immediately stuck back under the heap of pillows, "this is not your fault. It's the government's fault. The government that's becoming flabbier every day! Even if it were made up of women, it would act more decisively."

"Listen a minute, Grandpa. Since a complaint can't be filed . . ."

"We talked about it, discussed it," the old man's son put in

23

at this point. "Don't think we didn't consider taking strong action. But granted that strong action seemed indicated in this case, what would we have gained by it? Nothing, except that we'd also be coming down to their level and losing what is essentially our own character."

"Jail! That's what needed!" the old man began to grumble. "Jail!" But he grumbled it so softly as to make it seem that either he was afraid of exaggerating or else he wanted to keep utterly for himself the joy with which his imagination had bodied forth the image of the entire Villa family, in handcuffs, their heads low, as they were led out of the Project one by one. And they're the ones, holy God, who would spit on us first of all! Because at the right moment, religion must defend itself in every way possible, swords and gallows included. If it really means to defend itself!

"I understand. In short, we've acted like rabbits again. The only thing you were capable of doing was to draw up another poster. Isn't that so? Another poster that will proclaim to everybody what they've done. Another poster on which at a certain point 'shit' will have to be written, and 'shit' of course, our democracy, on the other hand, doesn't permit us to write. Is that so, or isn't it?"

"But, Grandpa, try to understand."

"The real misfortune, my dear children, is that I can't move any more. Because if I could get up, I'd show you how to get rid of those bastards. Fists, that's what's needed, not posters! Fists!" And with the words the old man lifted his right fist, clutching the rosary beads, from under the blankets and extended it toward his son and grandson. "Then, at your leisure, but at your leisure, the rest!" he concluded, letting his arm fall back on the blankets.

His fury and agitation had caused a yellowish veil of sweat to issue from his temples, under his nostrils, and all around his head and neck.

"Calm down, Papa."

24

"We've told you from the start not to get all upset over those scoundrels." Luigi said "scoundrels" trying to load the word with a sense of indignation which his nature, however, seemed unable to lend it.

But the old man showed no signs of calming down. Now, not only his arm but his entire body was trembling as if in the impossibility of doing what he felt impelled to do.

"Besides, you know as well as we do that we can never win around here."

"Yes, yes, I don't deny it," rumbled the old man, over whom the grandson was hovering to dry off his sweat. "But in my opinion, the good Lord would be quite willing to see a little less Communion and a little more courage!"

At these words the younger Olivas, father and son, stared at each other for an instant, gripped by similar feelings of shock and compassion. Shock because of the force and violence that the old man showed despite his years, and which, perhaps, deeply within themselves they also would have liked to possess; and compassion because—they thought—this odd conception of religion could only be the result of old age.

In reality, things were quite different. In fact, from his youth, the spring on which old Oliva's spirit rested had been the idea of the Christian soldier of the Gospels, armed with sword, revolver, and cannon. From then on, he had bet everything on that. "I say if we've got blood in our veins and a desire to trade blows, the good Lord alone must have given them to us!"

And so he had been the first to be astonished that only a shadow of so much ardor had been passed on to his son. Oh, he was a practicing Catholic, scrupulous, even too much so, at least for old Oliva, who'd always done things a bit more loosely; but as for determination, courage, guts . . . zero. So much so as to induce the old man to believe that his son's character came entirely from his wife. A pious soul, God knows, and if she hadn't gone to Paradise who else would have gone there! Pious and extra-pious. But too docile. Too meek, that was it.

25

Of course in a woman, well, even an excess of virtue might be considered an advantage, but when it came to a man!

The doubt never brushed his mind that had his wife not been as she was, then not the Ave Maria but plates would have been flying about in his house, and perhaps blasphemies. His grandson's boyhood, on the other hand, had given him cause for hope, profound hope, at least until his return from military service. Because from then on, against all logical expectations, Luigi had completely withdrawn into himself. A priest, in short. But one of those priests of whom, should you see him, you would say: "If I were His Eminence, I'd send that fellow off to serve as chaplain in some institute of nuns." And instead of toughening him up and sending him home a man right down to the bone, the Third Artillery Regiment of Campania, the Fifth Group of Salerno, Nocera Inferiore, and Santa Maria Capua Vetere had made him wan and cowering. As if he had performed his military service in a Jesuit institute for spiritual exercises! Pious, extra-pious, those things, sure, but they couldn't take the place of everything. Not the way the world was going. A world in which it would be necessary to empty out all these spiritual institutes, sell them, and put cinemas, theaters, television sets in their place. Gyms, football stadiums, not pulpits and preachers! People aren't going to church any more? Well then, go outside, out into the piazzas, the bars, the streets! Go out with radios, microphones, loud-speakers, and, if necessary, trumpets and gallows!

Thus, during his illness, what caused him suffering was not his ailments—which he'd always mentioned only to a select few, and which in a certain sense made him feel proud—but being absent from the great battles: the elections. He'd been able to see only two of them. Then, no more, except for the few carried on down there in the courtyard of the Housing Project by his friends and enemies. Besides, what illusions could anyone have about the Housing Project? Except for them, the Oliva family, even those who perhaps weren't C.P. members now would make their little cross alongside the hammer and sickle at the right moment, and then, amen.

Four years ago, however, the evening when the Communists had organized their celebration right there beneath his window, when he could no longer stand listening to all that blasphemy vomiting forth out of the mouth of the microphone, he had found enough strength in himself to jump out of bed, go to the window, lean out, and shout: "Antichrists! Swine!" And it didn't matter that he'd had a collapse a little while after, during the broadside of whistling that greeted his invective, and fallen to the floor before his son and daughter-in-law, who were just suffering around the table, could get to him.

And, furthermore, he simply couldn't understand why his grandson should read so much, considering the results, apart from the fact that it was ruining his complexion. If he didn't come from a family in which everyone had passed seventy, and passed it almost always on horseback, one might have doubts about his health. But the day he had to drop all these meetings, books, newspapers, posters, and fight with his fists, how would he make out with those beasts? That gang had to be cut down with an ax, not with humbug! And this was another thing he couldn't understand. True, if God the Father made him like that, he must have had his reasons.

In God's place, he would have put Christians together with a little more nerve and backbone. But since they were what they were, a good injection of courage every morning wouldn't do them any harm. Why, just look at him! No amount of colic, bronchitis, physical collapse could break his will. And why? Certainly it was God's will, but it was his own will, too.

"Bah, so it means we'll be seeing, rather you'll be seeing, those posters again," the old man said to his son and grandson, who, embarrassed by his reactions, continued to remain silent. Soon after, Enrica called both men to the table; the soup was ready, in fact, already ladled out.

"As far as I'm concerned, I tell you they're doing fine . . . no, wonderful!" Carlo Villa shouted, raising his glass and gulping down whatever wine remained. Then, grabbing a small roll from his right, he began gobbling down mouthfuls, one after the other.

"At least, by forcing us to look at their faces printed all over the place, people will understand that it's time to get rid of those pigs of gentlemen!" he added. "After all, is there freedom of speech, or isn't there? Besides, under this government of priests, our mouths are shut plenty!"

"In things of importance, yes. But in this, no, you just make matters worse keeping your mouth open."

"You're kidding yourself! This rottenness, my dear family, sooner or later makes everyone rot. Them first of all. From morning to night they show us those swinish faces of priests, gentlemen, thieves! They show us their shindigs, scandals, whorehouses! Fine! Wonderful! In this way, when we can't stand it any longer, we'll go grab them and throw it all back in their mugs. Then a shot for each of them and the world'll start to be a little cleaner!" Now, Carlo had a fork in his hand and was staring dully at it. When he had put it back on the table he added: "And to be frank about it, it doesn't please me particularly to know that Antonio is running around with those pigs, just because he's a boxer."

"But Antonio's doing it because he has to," the mother said.

"Could be," Carlo shot back. "But I don't want them to make him sink lower than he is. Don't you see? He doesn't seem one of us any more. Oh sure, he's proud of being champ, proud of being first! Don't think I don't understand those things! But that's no reason for forgetting everything else, including the fact that he sweats, works hard, and swears all day.

Try asking him if between a match and a Party meeting he'd choose the meeting. . . ."

The discussion which the father had started about the display of carryings-on, luxuries, and wasted millions printed week after week in the papers and illustrated magazines, was almost immediately squashed by Carlo. A subject of far greater interest to him, it was clear from the start, had to be brought before the family—especially since Antonio was absent—namely, the way in which his brother was going.

"Now listen, since he's not here, because he's probably eating out again with that gang of I don't know what. They're exploiting him for his muscles. Muscles that he owes you and Mother, first bringing him into the world, and then working like dogs to bring him up."

"He's right," Liberata said, speaking up for the first time, her voice hard and pitiless. "Things like that shouldn't happen in our family."

"But what's happening?" the mother shouted. "And suppose he's exploiting *them*?"

"Exploiting them, sure!"

"Oh, you can be sure about that. Antonio isn't the kind of kid who'll play the sucker."

"You're deluding yourself. Exploit people who up to now have done nothing but exploit us! Morini, for instance, that swine Villapizzone who doesn't let anyone . . ."

"Now, what's Morini got to do with it?" the mother broke in hurriedly. "I don't even know who he is."

"He's the president of the organization where Antonio went to join up just the other evening."

"So what? What should he do, according to you? Change him?"

"Join up elsewhere! As if we don't also have gyms! Besides," Carlo added after hesitating slightly, "it doesn't mean very much, but he might have told us, first you, her, me . . . It's true he's older, but just the same he knows that I understand more than he does about these things."

"About these things and everything," Liberata said, speaking up for the second time.

The obstinacy with which the girl supported her brother, even before knowing his opinions and thoughts, was mostly a self-contradiction since it revealed her own absolute lack of personal convictions, not to speak of character. It was true that convictions, in this family, were more or less the same. But among father, mother, brothers, there were differences of opinion that sometimes burst into genuine dissensions when the talk touched on crucial issues. On those occasions Liberata had no choice but to oppose now her father, now her mother, now Antonio; and this she did, simply and solely to defend Carlo's proposals and position. As soon as he opened his mouth, it was: "Carlo's right." Or: "Correct." Or else: "Absolutely correct." And if the others persisted she became furious, even going so far as to shout that the truth of whatever Carlo was maintaining was proved by the fact that he was the only one among all of them who had been entrusted by the leadership with an important and specific duty. And she went on shouting even though she knew it hurt her father, who had always been ambitious to achieve what his son had won so easily and with such unanimous approval.

"Well then, what are we supposed to do?" the father asked.

"Call him aside and speak to him."

"Wouldn't it be better to wait?" the mother interrupted.

"Wait for what?" Liberata said.

"Wait till he's really done something or at least said something," the mother explained.

"Ah, but why, if you think your son's about to go under, why wait till he's under, before warning him?"

"But who's about to go under?"

"He is!"

30

"And if Carlo says so . . ." Liberata said, getting up from the table to carry the pile of dishes to the drainboard of the sink.

"Oh, now he's become a new Togliatti, eh?" the mother grumbled.

"Who said anything about Togliatti? It's only that Carlo understands some things better than all of us put together."

"Also about that business of the posters?" the mother rejoined.

"Especially that!" Liberata said.

"In other words, according to you, it was a good thing to have everyone say that we ripped them up, and that we don't even know what freedom is."

"Exactly!" Liberata shouted.

"As far as that's concerned," Carlo said, suddenly banging his fist on the table, "I'm willing to take a laxative just to shit all over those treacherous posters again!"

There was a long silence.

"Listening to you," the father said, "it would seem that I don't even exist. Let me say something, based on a lot of personal experience. Because when being on our side, or at least not on theirs, meant jail, you were still crapping in your pants!"

Liberata, who had finished cleaning off the table and was turning on the faucets, looked toward Carlo to receive her cue. When she saw that her brother was signaling her to stay calm, she struck the pile of silverware, which tinkled sharply and ominously. Then without a word, she continued cleaning up.

"What, exactly, do you know?" the father asked Carlo, who was slowly leafing through the paper. "Let's talk about it a bit, just the two of us, but calmly. Then we'll decide what should be done."

Understanding that her husband would like some privacy, the wife got up from her place and walked toward the sink, ready to take the plates, soup dishes, glasses, and silverware from her daughter, and dry them. Amidst these tasks she thought again of how her husband had shouted the day she had

31

decided on the name of her first-born. "Antonio?" he'd shouted. "Why Antonio? Because that was your brother's name? As for me, I've never liked saints' names." But she insisted and finally her husband had surrendered. "Well, if you feel so strongly about it, all right, let's call him Antonio. But I'm afraid it won't bring him luck." Thus, she hadn't dared put forward any suggestions for the two following children, and they had been named, one, Carlo, not for the saint but for the author of *Das Kapital,* and the other Liberata, because there was no liberty in Italy that year. A name that they meant as a symbol of hope and rebellion.

22

The storm ended, the air immediately became dirty, dusty, heavy again over the city buildings. In the outskirts, however, it still retained its exciting after-shower freshness, and it would certainly have done so all night had not the Pero refinery begun its slow but inexorable infiltration of smells.

It was a stench that managed to infect and corrupt all the air in short order. Thus the flame which, flaring to the north, could be seen from the highest windows of the Housing Project as well as from all the smallest houses and dairy farms of Roseria, Vialba, Musotto, and Certosa, became the signal for a nauseating and maleficent fire repeated every evening, as if every evening those poor huge barracks heaped one on top of the other had to become immersed in mire and mud instead of peaceful sleep.

That someone in the Project was staying up at that hour quarreling, everyone understood from certain words that were rising like shrieks. But it became certain only when a door suddenly banged and above the bang a woman's voice, out of control, began screaming:

32

"A swine, yes! And let him keep his vices to himself! Because if I see them together again I'm going to the police! Understand?"

Then a furious clatter down the stairs, another bang, another door slamming with the same violence as before.

"Well, here we go! No sleep again tonight," Redenta said, her nerves drawn taut by the unresolved storm, and by headache. She had struggled even more than usual to get some sleep. And since she'd understood immediately whose voice it was, she immediately wondered what could possibly have happened except Schieppati seeing her son in company with Cornini, or something like that.

She could hear the rumble of a car drawing closer and closer and slowing up, until it stopped completely at the end of the hedge surrounding the garden.

"It can rain and rain and more than rain," Redenta said, feeling an upsurge of envy and sickening anger as soon as the car had stopped. "Even if the fields turn into sewers they'll find a way to carry on their filthiness, if they've got to!" Because at night when no one could see, or even guess at her thoughts, Redenta's defenses gave way to an utter and desperate weakness. Then, those instincts and desires that she'd managed to keep quietly in the depths of her heart during the day floated to the surface and took command over everything.

23

"In a urinal, they had to see me go into a urinal! And all because of that bastard!"

Finally up the stairs, Schieppati had re-entered her house whiter than usual, her lips bloodless, her eyes tense and hallucinated. So great were her horror and scorn that as soon as she was inside she wanted to return to that wretched Cornini boy's mother, begin shouting at her again, and warn her to keep her mouth tightly shut. "Because nobody has to know anything about what I've said here, understand?" But thinking about it again, she convinced herself that it would be absolutely unwise to go back there. In fact, aside from the humiliation of resuming that argument, it surely wasn't to Cornini's interest to spread the rumor and so she would keep her mouth tightly shut. Now, Schieppati looked at the pile of laundry she had left there to be put in order, and she sat down heavily, brusquely, put on her glasses, took the first jersey, and began twisting it this way and that to see where it would be best to start mending.

Though nobody in the Project, except for Redenta, would have thought it possible of her, so obviously a dedicated wife and mother, the truth was that from time to time the poor woman was exasperated to the point of cursing the days when she had submitted to her stupid ignorant husband's sensual greed and as a result had put into the world all those children —seven of them. And seven children meant seven mouths to fill, seven bodies to clothe, seven heads to control. Control, yes —but how? Even if one did all one could to keep track of their doings and see that they bettered themselves, there'd always be someone, two floors up, who would lead them into shamefulness, vice, jail.

She cursed herself and that husband of hers who—God help her—might at least have tried to better their situation. But no such luck. He'd been a mason when the first child came. He was still a mason when they got the last. And he would remain a mason as long as he could stand up straight.

On the other hand, it seemed that everything and everyone conspired to push Sandrino, the oldest of the seven, onto the path he'd taken. A path which at first she'd only suspected, but now, ever since her brother had given her the fine news of what he'd seen, now she knew with certainty.

"You're mistaken, and very much mistaken. If my Luciano is even aware your Sandrino exists, it's because he sees him around here. As for the rest of it, if he really wants to get it out of his system, let him go take up with those delinquents in the Park, because I'm told that's where he hangs out day and night."

"Sure, and your Luciano frequents the houses of kings and princes, instead!" Thus in snatches, that conversation of a little while ago came back to Schieppati's mind, proving how right she had been not only in thinking that the Cornini boy would set her son on that road, but also revealing the depth to which he had sunk. Seventeen, barely seventeen, and already come to that. But having reached that point, what could she do? Snatch him from that road, when fate itself seemed obstinately bent on not letting him find a job that was a real job? And then, once one has found this way of making out and that source of income, how could he now be persuaded to roll up his sleeves and go to work?

As her needle slipped in and out of the weave of the jersey, mending the tear that had been ripping along the bottom, Signora Schieppati asked herself how she could possibly have given birth to a son so different from the others. Because if one thought about it, the others were also different one from the other, but different with regard to the color of their hair or eyes, their character or the shape of their faces, but as for the rest . . .

And now there they were, sleeping away, all six of them. Four in the first room. Four, but with a place left vacant, since Sandrino hadn't come home yet. Better not to think of where and with whom he was now, since if she let her thoughts run along that way . . . Oh, and that day with the storm and all!

"You can just imagine, Edvige, whether I would have the courage to come here and tell you something like this if I weren't absolutely sure. I saw him myself, with my own eyes, while I was making my last delivery. He was in the Boschetti, the thickets. I recognized him by his jersey. Then I also saw his face. Then in order not to be seen, I hid behind a shrub. They went on talking awhile; then they got into the car. Seemed to be a Como license. And him, that swine, about fifty years old."

Poverty. That was the true cause, the true blame for everything. Poverty and hunger on the one hand. And nothing to do, and money and vices on the other!

They ought to be picked up, shaken loose of everything they had, and throttled, those swine who with their money ruin even those who don't want it. Poverty, she said and repeated to herself, and hunger. The same poverty and the same hunger that constrained the other six to eat the way they were eating and sleep the way they were sleeping: sprawled out on the mattresses like animals being carried off in carts to the slaughterhouse, and the blankets and sheets so grimy and greasy it made one sick just to come near them.

24

After riding around in Morini's car in company with the other three boys, Binda among them, Antonio had returned all excited, weary but happy, so that he didn't foresee the reception awaiting him.

Scarcely had he entered when Carlo stood up from the table, where he was reading the last number of *Rinascita,* and stared at him, darkly, severely.

"At last!" he said.

"Why?" Antonio replied, setting on the table the metal valise that accompanied him from training session to training session every night.

"I have to talk to you."

"Well, go ahead and talk. I'm here. But try to get it over with fast because it's late."

"All right, I'll start. Where've you been? Come on now, speak up."

"Where have I been? At the gym."

"Is that the truth?"

"Look here," Antonio replied, pointing to the little metal valise on the table.

"Oh well, as far as that goes, it could also be a dodge."

"A dodge? Why a dodge?"

A brief silence, in which two or three pages of the magazine nervously rustled and the theme of a song faintly sounded in the air.

"And who'd you come back with? We might at least know that?" Carlo said.

"With the president."

"You mean that swine Morini."

"Oh, that's how you put it?" Antonio replied. Then, seizing his valise and walking toward his room, "Good night," he added.

"Antonio," Carlo said. "Listen, Antonio . . ."

"What should I listen to? You know as well as I do that we haven't seen things eye to eye for quite a while around here."

"Naturally, as long as you continue to pal around with characters like your friends in the gym and their leaders. But you're forgetting who you are, and the kind of family you come from, and the kind of ideas your father, mother, and sister have."

"I'm not forgetting anything."

"No? Then explain to me why you're never seen at Party headquarters."

"Because I have other things to do."

"You see!"

"See what? What are you trying to see? Look here, are you leading the life you want? Yes? Well, I'm doing what I want to do. Or is your idea of freedom the same as the priests'?"

"Antonio!" Carlo shouted, his voice suddenly becoming harsh.

"Now just listen. Let those who are sleeping sleep and let's go to bed too. If you really want to, we can talk about this thing more comfortably another time."

"No, we'll talk about it now!"

"Then talk. But without shouting, if possible."

"Exactly. Without shouting," the mother said, suddenly opening the door and unexpectedly but determinedly breaking into the conversation.

"You see, you see who's your protector?" Carlo shouted, caught off balance by this unlooked-for interruption. Then, turning to his mother:

"Well, it's certainly not for nothing that you come from a family of seminarists!"

"You better watch your tongue, Carlo! Because no matter what your ideas, I won't allow you to insult our mother!"

Antonio had drawn close to his brother and seemed hanging over him with the full bulk of his weight.

"Because if this is what your papers and magazines are teaching you, then you'd be better off without reading them! And besides, am I by any chance doing anything against you and your beliefs? Am I?"

Carlo, who for a moment had seemed almost bewildered, now turned and moved away toward the window.

"Well, just explain to me how you can possibly manage to hang around with that crowd?"

"I have to. For my career," Antonio replied, very sure of himself. "Besides, you know how I think. We only live once and we've got to live the best we can."

"Oh, and what about corruption, betrayal?"

"But who's corrupting? Who's betraying?"

"I'd like to believe at least that you know what's being said about that swine, your president."

"So?"

"So, so!" Carlo replied.

"Antonio's right," the mother interrupted. "If it's necessary to do these things, to get where he wants to . . ."

"Furthermore," the older Villa brother burst out, "I wouldn't claim that everybody enjoys ripping up posters!"

"Antonio! It's time to let up on that business of the posters!

38

I've told you too that if necessary I'm ready to do the same thing again for the rest of my life. Because, remember, I'm not like you. I believe in my ideas and the ideas my father taught me, and I'll believe in them to the end!"

At that moment, Liberata appeared in the gap of the door left open by the mother. Paler than the whiteness of her nightshirt, her jaws set, her eyes glinting, she glanced at Antonio for an instant, then said:

"That's right. To the end."

25

It was already past one in the morning and the air was heavy and unbreathable with the stench emanating from the Pero works, mixed with the humidity. Sandrino stepped off the tram, hurriedly said good night to the two friends with whom he had strolled about in the Park before and after the storm, and began to walk home. He felt utterly worn out, dulled, and these feelings were hardly compensated for by what he had in his pocket, assuring him not only something to eat for a day or so, but also enough for a new pair of trousers, exactly like those he'd seen just after the storm at Carrobbio in Araldo's window.

Rapidly crossing Via Aldini, he reached the Project. At the entrance he saw Candida being embraced by someone whom he couldn't make out, except for his shoulders and the motorcycle nearby. He only heard the girl murmuring:

"Nothing. Don't worry. It's someone from here, one of those who had better keep quiet."

Shrugging off this insinuation, he crossed the kitchen gardens. As he was about to open the door, down the toilet pipe there fell so thunderous a clamor as to lead one to think half the building was going down with it.

"Good-by," he said, as if greeting a friend going off forever, and entered.

The light filtering along the door had already prepared him for what was certainly going to happen; and when he went in, he was blinded. He hadn't yet managed to get his bearings when his mother glared at him and signaled to him to stay right where he was, still and silent.

"Decent folk are asleep in bed at this hour.

"Well?" she added, approaching close enough to smell his breath and, together with his breath, his wet clothes. "And just look at that face of yours! Look at it! If you go on like this, you'll wind up in some TB sanatorium."

"So what if I wind up with TB!" Sandrino replied, shrugging his shoulders.

"All right, now do you care to tell me where you've been and with whom? Because as soon as I know the names of those delinquents I'm reporting them to the police and having them all locked up!"

"What names do you want me to give you?"

"It just doesn't seem possible that a son could hear his mother make charges like that and not burst out crying, not feel ashamed." Now Schieppati was speaking in muffled tones, so that no one might hear, and yet her voice was full of grief and indignation. "Now at last I know exactly what's going on. Look here, I can tell you everything. And I can tell you exactly and in detail."

"Well, go on, tell it."

"Don't act like that, Sandrino, don't act like that to your mother."

"Go on, say it, I'm listening. I'm listening to hear what you know."

"Yesterday, one of your uncles . . ."

"One of my uncles? And what makes you think I care a damn about one of my uncles?"

40

"One of your uncles, Uncle Mario, yes, him. Yesterday, toward evening . . ."

"Toward evening?"

"He saw you."

"He saw me? Where?"

"In the Boschetti."

"In the Boschetti?"

"Yes, in the Boschetti, while you were making a deal with someone."

"Don't make me laugh."

"Ah, I make you laugh! Well then, listen. Leaving with that . . . It makes me sick just to say it, sick! Well, leaving there you got into that degenerate's car. Enough? Want to hear more? It was a car with a Como license plate. Is that true or isn't it?" At this point the mother, who felt she was running the risk of losing her son's affection, perhaps forever, by such a statement, stared fixedly at Sandrino as if to prevent him from escaping.

"And even if it were true, what are you trying to say?"

"That you disgust me and if you don't quit all this, you see the door? Well, take it, get out, and don't ever set your foot in this house again! I mean never again! Because if you want to ruin your own life, why, go ahead. But I've got six others to think about. You understand? Six others!"

There was a long pause. The woman began trembling and twisting her fingers: "Oh, what wrong have I committed to deserve a son like you! What have I done?"

"Ask Father. Don't you remember what he shouted in my face two or three months ago? 'I have no more money to give you. If you can manage to make a living by yourself, fine, otherwise, go your own way.' And since nobody's ever found a job for me, I've had to make a living with whatever I've got at my disposal."

"Sandrino," the woman murmured again.

"Leave me alone. I'm so tired I can hardly stand on my feet. I'm soaked. Can't you see? Besides, if I really disgust you, all you have to do is say the word, and I'll leave at once. I know, now, it's not very hard to find someone who'll give you not only grub but a bed too. All you have to do is change from time to time, like in the hotels."

Sandrino had not yet finished speaking when his mother, racked with sobs, collapsed against the table. At the blow, the last jerseys, the last stockings, the last handkerchiefs that remained to be mended fell to the floor.

For a moment the boy looked at his mother, then, without saying another word, went into the bedroom. And there, the sight of all those bodies sprawled out or huddled on the beds, emanating a warm revolting smell, filled him even more than any other evening with a sense of pity and rebellion.

"Bloody noses now, too!" he said, when, sitting on the bed to take off his shoes, he saw that the brother with whom he shared the cot had left some reddish stains on the pillow, and another stain on the sheet tracing all his movements. "That too!"

Just at that moment, Luciano entered the kitchen garden enclosure. Once again he had spent an evening in company with G.P., a hotel owner whose acquaintance he had made twenty days before at the Lirico gate. Once again G.P. had taken him to the apartment at No. 43 Via C. and tried to persuade him to do what up until then he'd never wanted to accept from anyone. But although the offer had been higher than the other evenings, Luciano had refused.

"Oh, that's how the price is raised! And who tells you I'll stay in the running?"

"Who? Your face."

"Bah, that's what you think. . . ."

Luciano's step resounded in the stair well as if it were issuing from the depths of the earth.

Lying in bed, unable to sleep, still preyed upon by nightmares and desperate thoughts, Redenta heard him. "That's him, for sure, that poor bastard!" she said.

42

In the Project resounded the groan of a door, then a scraping of footsteps. Then nothing.

26

Born and raised in that neighborhood, Redenta remembered everything about the Project, and she remembered it with the preciseness and power of her remarkable memory; because once she had seen or heard a thing, there within her head it remained fixed and locked up, as in a safe, fixed and locked forever. Here were the days when she romped playing with her friends on what was then nothing but a meadow. Here were the Sundays when she went with her father, mother, and uncles to watch the progress of what had become the principal event in the area. A title, furthermore, which it deserved, inasmuch as it was the first real people's housing project to be built in the area, towering over the small country dwellings, so that everyone all around there was led to believe that it would become a model, the model, rather, for future workers' housing, even for people who weren't workers. But now, thirty-five years later, here it was: a wreck. Oh sure, drinking water and toilets had been put in; she had not complained then and was not complaining now about that: every apartment had been provided with its sink and bathroom. And who could deny that at *that* time, 1923, *that* was something? Except that the landlords, or rather the syndicate, was absentee, and so they had allowed things to run down year after year, just go to pieces. Thus, already at the time of the Abyssinian war, the one that her Andrea had just dodged by a hair, houses so much better constructed had been put up around there, and the Project had gone downhill so much, that from a pre-eminent position it had descended halfway down the scale. Then, finally, from that halfway place,

43

after the war—not Abyssinian this time but the whole world—
it ended right at the bottom. That is, it became the *refugium
peccatorum* of the neighborhood, as priests and monks cried
from the pulpits. The tenants also, like the walls, the plumbing,
the roof, shutters, toilets, and drinking water, had gone downhill
more or less and ended up nothing.

And that was why Redenta derived no pleasure or emotion
from these episodes which she happened to remember from
time to time, for no apparent reason. Here she was in those
far-off days running like a stupid little fool. Here she was hiding. Here she was flinging herself down on the meadow. Here
she was being stared at by her first beaux, little boys with scraped
knees . . . Yes, because after all life heaps up and forces one
to bear so many misfortunes on one's shoulders, that no one
would willingly turn back, even if he could. Just one of these
Lacrimarum valle is enough! Oh, more than enough! Instead,
the Vales of Tears multiply. Multiply until the day is inevitably cursed when father and mother had the fine idea of bringing you into the world.

A fine idea if, on top of it all, what happened to her doesn't
happen to you. Because why wasn't a poor devil like her Andrea
given a bit of spine? Are you a man? Well, then, get moving!
Do you think you can go on fooling yourself that the bosses
won't need you too, some day or other? Well then, get going,
have fun, have fun while there's still time. Have fun and give
fun to one who needs it.

Fun indeed—poor fool that she was! Waiting, waiting until
your man takes you, embraces you, presses you close, kisses
you, lets you know what it's like to be drunken with love, that
love which makes everyone lose whatever brains they have!
When someone is said to be serious, you've got a long wait! So
time passes, the draft notice arrives, the train leaves, the ship
draws away from the wharf, and "Good-by, good-by, my sweet,
the army's on its way."

And with the army the dreams of becoming a wife, of having

44

a family, a house, in short, of becoming someone yourself. A nice burst of machine-gun fire right in the guts, and down you go! Oh, yes, he might even have called out her name. But what use was it, then? He should have done it before, because then . . . Then, what could he have hoped for? That she would run down there and lift his head so that if he really had to breathe his last, he would breathe it right there, in her arms? If at least they had left her that one frail consolation. Instead, nothing. The news had arrived when her Andrea, besides having kicked off, had already begun to rot. A lovely ditch on the mountainside, a lovely cross above him, and then down comes the wind, down comes the snow, down comes the storm, down comes everything! Not even a spot one might visit on Sundays and say a requiem and bring a flower! Not even that much had been left her!

Must she, then, with that fine beginning and the subsequent likelihood that everyone would go to rot one day or another—must she accept the task of preparing, holding in her hands, pounding, cooking, and then swallowing all those slices of veal, beef, and roast her brother insisted on?

Leaning on the windowsill, Redenta thought about all this, and while thinking, she watched the last tenants entering the enclosure, cross the kitchen gardens, climb the stairs, and disappear into the house. Then, from the other side of the fence, the poster squad began to move forward like guards executing an order given by God knows who. The poster squad was made up of two young men about twenty years old, trailed by a trio of older men who seemed to be their protectors and advisers. Of the two young men, one carried a ladder, the other a roller and a pail.

"Here we go," said Redenta when she realized what was up. "The same old story! As if we can fill our stomachs and pay our rents with these posters and the childishness printed all over them!"

Meanwhile, the poster squad was reaching the end of the garden. When they finally stood in front of the house, one of the three protectors stepped forward and said to the younger men: "Here. Put it up here. This is the spot."

27

The first to enter the Project after the five men had gone, and consequently the first to see the posters, was Liberata.

Drops and blobs of paste were slowly oozing down from the posters and the wall. Looking out the window, Redenta Restelli saw the Villa girl enter, start to cross the garden court, and then suddenly stop.

"Filthy bastards!" the girl muttered, grinding her teeth, while a chill ran along her spine. "Now I suppose they think they've got their revenge?"

A moment of hesitation. Then a step forward, just enough to read them clearly. All around her, happy thoughtless children continued playing their final games and races of the day.

"Oh, that's how it is!" Liberata added, as soon as she had read one of the posters in its entirety. "What else could they write? Oh, I wish I had you here, Antonio, so we could read all these dirty lies together!" Then, telling herself that it would be enough just having her mother, that softy, here, she was swallowed up in the stair well.

Redenta, who had been motionlessly spying on the Villa girl's movements up to then, muttered: "That's it! Now the world blows up. Because this certainly isn't going to be the end of it."

"What! That's the end of it? No. This doesn't settle a damned thing!" Liberata shouted, twisting her fingers as if they were all nerves. "Just wait till Carlo comes home, then you can tell me what good is all your advice to be calm!"

"God willing," the mother replied, "when Carlo arrives it will be so dark that he'll no longer be able to read anything."

"But why do you talk like that? Whose side are you on? What are you driving at?"

"The only side I have to defend is the peace of my family."

"How? By spitting on our ideas?"

"I'm not spitting on anything. You're the ones who are getting yourselves criticized by everybody with this business of the posters! Don't you understand that's all they're waiting for, so that later they can say we're more fascist than the fascists?"

"Why do you believe all this rot? Well, go ahead and believe it. That way, within a few years we'll have thirty Mussolinis here instead of one. And everyone with a cross and a pot of holy water on hand. Besides, you're talking that way because you haven't seen what they've printed. Filthy lies, lies, lies! But with all the propaganda at their disposal, all those lies will end up in everybody's heads, even those who should be on our side. Did you really listen to what Carlo said last night? They've taken over everything: press, radio, television. Everything, those thieves! Everything!"

"All right, I don't deny it. But at least try to imagine what's going to happen if, when they wake up tomorrow, they find their posters torn off again? We'll have all the trouble, nobody else. And all because of your mania of being extremists, extremists even when it's not necessary. Look at Carlo. If it weren't that they can't find another one like him on the job, even if they paid in gold, they would have fired him a hundred times!"

"Sure. But that's as it should be. They'd like to fire him because he's a Communist? Well, they can't, because he does his job better than anyone else. It's a right he's earned."

"And what about me? Haven't I earned the right to do everything possible to calm all of you down? Because—you'd better listen well to this—because if I boiled over the way all of you do, everything around here would blow up."

"And it would be about time!" Liberata replied, beginning to shift nervously about.

There was a brief silence in the kitchen. Liberata stooped to pick up the vegetable basket from under the sink.

"All the same," she said, "those printed pieces of paper aren't going to stay on the walls of our house very long. If no one else decides to do anything about it, fine, that means I'll rip them off with these hands here."

"And when you've ripped them off?"

"I'll go about with my head higher and my conscience cleaner."

29

When old Oliva heard the news about the posters, he wasn't the least bit pleased. Instead, he immediately warned his grandson against deluding himself that they'd remain pasted up very long.

"But this time, Grandpa, it's against their own interests to rip them off," Luigi replied.

"Well, let's see what they do. But if they tear them off this time also, then it seems to me you can't look on any more. File charges, that's all. And charges that'll get all five of them hauled off together."

At that point of the dialogue between the old man and his grandson, the excited voices of several women rose from the courtyard. Both of them, and the son and daughter-in-law, who were in the kitchen, realized at once that the squabble had to do with the subject they were discussing.

"Listen, Luigi. Listen to what they're saying," the old man said. "I think they're talking about the posters."

Actually, the women weren't talking. They were yelling, cursing, swearing.

"Instead of printing up all this paper, why don't they use the money to put up houses and make it possible for us to lead a less miserable life!"

"Right! Good for you! That's the way to talk!" a bitter cutting voice shouted, rising above the others, a voice that old Oliva immediately recognized as Liberata's. As soon as she had finished preparing the vegetables, she'd gone downstairs to incite her fellow tenants.

"And you know what you ought to do so that everybody should know how you feel about it? Spit on them, on all these filthy lies, just like I'm spitting on them!" she shouted even more violently than before.

At that moment the old man's eyes seemed ablaze with a sulphurous light.

"Spit! Did you hear that, Luigi? That miserable girl said spit?" he muttered with whatever small voice he could muster.

But, at Liberata's proposal, the discussion down in the court got so loud that the old man's anger couldn't be heard.

"Yes, spit! Spit all over these scraps of paper and those traitors upstairs on the third floor," Meroni said, "because they're the ones who cook up all these things around here."

"They call us fascists when they know very well who sent our sons to war and had them blessed before sending them!"

"Yes! That's it! Since they couldn't bless them afterward, when they'd already become cannon fodder!"

At that point, struck by the reference, Redenta, who had been listening motionlessly until then, plunged into the discussion:

"Cannon fodder, yes! Cannons and slaughterhouses!" she yelled, her full bosom jutting over the windowsill. "As they did with my Andrea! Since they're not satisfied with treating us like worms, they'd like us to feed the worms beforetime!"

This unexpected but trenchant interruption, in which nerves, anger, indignation, and grief combined to lend her voice the power of a howl, at once caused the women to turn around and look up.

"Come down, come down, Redenta!" Liberata yelled. It didn't seem possible that Signorina Restelli too had decided to take her side so strongly. "Come down! So we can make a bonfire of all these sheets and burn them all up!"

The proposal for a bonfire spread through the group of women like the spark of a fire, almost as if the sunset which was now about to spread in the sky had enwrapped them all in its flames.

"A bonfire!" a woman at the right shouted.

"A bonfire!" shouted another at the left.

"And let's burn up this government of priests and thieves at the same time!"

"A bonfire! Yes, a bonfire!"

An instant, and that word shouted from mouth to mouth reached the old man's ears.

"What? A bonfire! They want to start a bonfire!?" he said abruptly. Then, shoving off the blankets with a motion of his hand: "Come here, get me a bathrobe! A robe, hurry! These damned women aren't going to light any bonfires, ever! A robe! I said a bathrobe!"

Son, daughter-in-law, and grandson rushed to the old man, who, despite the stitches in his side, was still trying to lift himself by his elbows and get off the bed.

"What are you up to, Papa?"

"Calm down, for heaven's sakes, calm down!"

50

"Don't kill yourself because of those four antichrists."

"Well, then, go down, the two of you! Go on! Get down there! Get down before they really start a bonfire!" And since his son and grandson seemed to be hesitating: "I said go downstairs! What are you waiting for? Is that all the guts you have?"

The two Olivas looked at each other for a moment longer, then slowly left the room. The daughter-in-law now straightened the sheets and covered the old body again, trying to calm him, now with words, now with caresses. But the old man continued grumbling in a thick-breathed raucous voice.

"They'd like to have my death also on their consciences. And they'll have it. Don't worry, they'll have it."

"But why get so excited about these things, Papa?" said the daughter-in-law. "They are just mad because they'll never be able to win enough . . ."

"Never! Never my foot! I'd like to see, in a little while, what's become of your 'never.'"

Meanwhile, Oliva, son, and Oliva, grandson, were getting to the bottom of the stairs. Redenta, who had come down just a little sooner, began to shout that it was right and more than right. Put an end to it.

"Anarchy, that's what's needed. I've always said it. Anarchy, anarchy, and still more!"

Sure of themselves, even if their faces were paler than usual, the two Oliva men went out the doorway and stopped in front of the group of women. There was a moment of silence in the courtyard. Then, as if obeying a command, one by one the women left their battle posts looking scornfully at the two men, as if they were passing in front of carrion.

Only Signora Balzani spoke, calling her son before deciding to follow the others.

"Come, Remigio, it's time to go home," she said. "I don't want you staying here and catching an infection from these saints. . . ." And tugging him along behind, she also disappeared beyond the vestibule, in the gloom of the staircase.

Only Liberata and Redenta remained there in front of the men of the Oliva family. But so venomously were they glaring at them that after a while both men preferred to go back in the house. No sooner had they turned their backs than Redenta Restelli leaned her bosom and head toward the wall and spat against it. Swiftly both men spun around.

"What's the matter?" Redenta cried. "I've a right to do that much, no? Especially since I'm more full of phlegm than a TB!"

At these words and the gesture that had preceded it, Liberata's face lighted up vividly. Her mouth, usually closed, opened in a smile of triumph. Then everything returned to normal.

30

"I certainly can't go down on an empty stomach to see what they've written!" Carlo said.

From the way in which her brother had received the news, it seemed to Liberata that something more serious than the posters was troubling him.

Returning from the Party headquarters when it was already late, Carlo had started to eat at once, and alone. Spoonfuls of the minestra that the old woman had tried to keep warm on the hot plate and which precisely for that reason had thickened into a kind of mush made up of rice, cabbage, beans, and potatoes. And between one spoonful and another, some chunks of bread and gulps of wine.

After a little while, when the last globs had been sopped up, Carlo pushed his soup plate to the right and began his questioning.

"Now you see, you who are always defending him," he said, turning to his mother.

52

"What do you mean? What's happened now?" the woman replied.

"He said No."

"What?" Liberata interrupted.

"He said No, no! So, why should I care about the posters when we are hatching traitors here among us, in our own home!"

"No? How come, no?" Liberata insisted.

"He said they won't allow him to fight for charities." A pause. Then: "Charities! That's what he called it! When it should be an honor for anyone to do something so that Party headquarters could look a little less run-down than they do now! So, at next week's celebration, when everybody will be doing something, he, a Villa, a Villa like you, like her, like me —not a thing. Business is business, he told me; contracts are contracts. And he told me that in front of everyone."

The mother kept silent. Only when her husband remarked that things couldn't go on like that, did she dare enter into the discussion.

"Now don't you start up, too," she said.

"Why shouldn't he also start up?" Liberata interrupted.

"I say, he needn't also start to go to extremes. Because there are already too many extremists in this house!"

"Who's being an extremist?" the father shot back. "I'm only trying to defend what have always been my beliefs."

"Well, then, defend yours and don't worry too much if someone else has others."

"But if that someone happens to be my son?"

"Exactly," Carlo repeated. "If that someone happens to be his son?" There was a long, heavy silence in the kitchen. The mother rose from her seat, took a plate, and set it before her son. Liberata took a salad dish from the closet and a plate with some slices of salami, three anchovies, and a chunk of Swiss cheese. Carlo poured himself half a glass of wine, which he then began to sip.

53

"Since we only live once . . ." the mother murmured after a while.

"So?" Liberata asked, mixing the salad leaves for the last time. "Since we only live once, does that give you the right to betray and cast dirt on others?"

"No. But the right to live a little less like thieves, yes. All that spite and envy, just because your brother is trying to make a success of his life!"

"It's obvious enough that he's trying," the father remarked. "But whether he's succeeding . . ."

"And what if he succeeds?" Carlo said. "They'll exploit him, that's all. Because that's been their system right along: exploit, exploit, and that's it. And with a bastard like Morini . . . Do you know how he finally managed with the sister of his favorite boy friend?"

"Are you talking about Binda?"

"About her, yes."

"Don't worry, I know all about it. She took a check, that's what finally happened. Then, to make the proverb come true, that money goes where money is, she married Garanzi, the butcher on Piazza Prealpi."

"As if a check could salve his conscience!" Carlo muttered.

"You're talking like a priest."

"As far as that goes," Liberata broke in shouting, "it's your family that's always hanging around the priests! The Villas have always hated the black cassocks. And they'll always hate them!"

"Hate! Hate! Can't you talk about anything else . . ."

"Oh sure! Just look at all the lovely benefits we've gained from all the love that's been preached at us till now from the pulpits!"

"Who's saying anything about love? I'm talking about self-interest."

"Which interest?" Liberata said. "That of losing one's own dignity in order to fatten the wallets of those who already have them stuffed full and more than full?"

54

"That remains to be seen."

"All right, you wait, then, wait. Then tell me about it."

Carlo was joylessly munching on a chunk of salami.

"His nerve," he said. "His nerve to come and say that to me in front of everyone! And everyone looking at me as if it were my fault! 'How come that you, who talk so much, couldn't even hold on to your own brother?' At that moment I felt like sinking into the ground for shame," he added. Then, after a brief pause, during which he glared at his mother: "For shame. Understand? And now I'm sorry I didn't have the guts to yell at him, yell right in front of everybody, that the person responsible for that betrayal was you, no one else but you! You, yes! Yes! You!" He was screaming now at the end.

"Come, now, Carlo, don't exaggerate," the father said, noticing that his wife had lowered her head and seemed on the verge of tears. "Tonight I'll talk to him myself."

"Tonight!" Liberata jeered. "Tonight's too late. It should have been done before."

"Tonight he'll tell you that he's signed a contract and that the terms are perfectly clear."

"As far as that goes, a contract can also be torn up!"

"Sure," Carlo replied. "If ideas matter more than fists. But since the only things that matter to him are fists, fists and glory . . ."

"Fine glory!"

"It's a glory just like any other," the mother dared observe, the tears streaming down her face. "Besides, if he believes in it . . ."

"If he believes in it?" Liberata burst out.

"That's enough!" the father interrupted at this point in a strong, determined voice. "Enough's enough. I said I'll speak to him tonight. Nothing's settled yet. It's possible he'll think it over and change his mind."

Carlo wiped his mouth with his napkin in a gesture of rage, took the glass, and gulped down the last mouthful.

"And what about those damned posters?" Liberata insisted.

"To the sink with you and get the dishwashing over with," the father replied.

"Well, if you don't want to think about it, I can always think about it," the girl continued, grabbing an apron and tying it around her waist.

There was a new silence. Then, as the spray of water began streaming down from the faucet onto the pile of plates and soup dishes, the mother's last snifflings and sobbings could be heard.

"Anything else?" Carlo asked, lifting his face toward his sister.

At these words the mother got up again, opened the cupboard doors, and took out a dish with three apples, two oranges, and half a pear.

"Eat this too. Do me a favor," she said, setting the fruit on the table. "If not, it'll go bad. . . ."

31

"They'll tear them off, for sure. They're just waiting till nobody's around, then, rip! with fingers and claws like the damned in hell!"

In the room's uncertain drowsiness, within the bed's humid yellow shadow, the mummy lay cuddled up within those thoughts as in a dream of victory. He couldn't understand why his son and grandson hadn't followed his advice, immediately going down into the courtyard, hiding behind the hedge, and waiting. "In that way, once you've caught them in the act, they won't be able to invent any alibis." But them, no. They wanted to go to Don Rinaldo's sermon, which he gave every Saturday night. So, those claws . . .

He saw them, right before his eyes, the claws of those antichrists, Carlo, Liberata, the father and mother of that Villa pack. Yes, he saw them as they tore into those posters, and then ripped down, down! Down another time, as the executioners had ripped down the body that once had hung poor and scorned on the cross.

"If only Our Father in Heaven would castigate them, and turn them all back against themselves, those shitty claws!" he said. At that moment a strong desire to shift position spread through his entire body. But warned by the pains that his rebellion a little while earlier had cost him, he didn't even dare attempt to move.

32

The posters. The bonfire they hadn't made, because just then those half-priests had come downstairs. Injustice. Poverty. The government. Hunger. True. All true. But Sandrino?

Three evenings now he hadn't come home. Three evenings she hadn't seen him. What was she to do? Go to the police and report it? When she spoke to her husband about it a little while ago he had forbidden her to do that. "What do you want to happen now? A scandal? He won't die of hunger, you can be sure. And if he really needs us, he'll be the first to remember that he has a home, a father, and a mother." But meanwhile they knew nothing. Where could he be? And where could he be spending all these days and nights?

Images of houses she didn't know, but which her imagination vividly conjured up into everything most inhuman and revolting. Rooms, beds, pillows, men undressing . . . And her Sandrino there, amidst all that. And if not there, where? In the Park between one avenue and another. At the Bastioni. At the Boschetti. Oh, why was life so beastly? Why did it make her suffer and mistreat her so?

Now where would she find the strength to stay here and

work? And after a while, where would she find the strength to go to bed if she still felt that emptiness in her heart? Sandrino, the one who'd made her tremble with pride and joy when he was born! No. Even if she wanted to, she wouldn't be able to sleep. Tonight also she would toss back and forth in the bed, holding her breath at every sound and every step she heard, or thought she heard, coming up the stairs, until her husband, weary of all her apprehensions, would tell her to go to hell. "If you can't sleep, at least let someone sleep who's got to be at the shop at eight o'clock tomorrow morning!" While she, on the other hand, would still be there at eight tomorrow morning, still in bed, wringing her hands. No. Staying there like that, waiting, waiting, just waiting—no, she couldn't.

So, although she was well aware of the risk, her mind reverted to the plan that seemed the only remaining solution. Act on it, wake up Vittorio, speak to him, he isn't that stupid, he must realize something. Then, taking advantage of the fact that her husband would have gone off to the bar, as he did every Saturday, she could leave the house, hop on a tram, and start looking right there in the Park, if it was there in the Park he spent most of the day. She would find someone. Some boy like himself, someone to speak with, to ask. He would have seen him. And if she questioned enough people, it wasn't possible that everyone would lie, it wasn't possible that some word wouldn't slip out.

As if by an act of will she would destroy the throng of images, shadows, fears that were assailing her (slowly the Park had become in her mind a lightless, bottomless ditch, a kind of hell), Signora Schieppati got up from her chair, went into her sons' room, woke Vittorio, and told him to watch over the others.

"You, at least, can help me," she concluded, looking fixedly at him.

Vittorio, who had more or less managed to open his eyes, replied:

"Go. Don't worry. I'll take care of everything here."

33

As soon as she stepped off the tram, she found herself facing
the huge shadows of the park. Tree trunks, plants, shrubbery,
and alongside the street lamps, figures stopping, and at once
walking off again. For a moment, Signora Schieppati hesitated.
Was he really in this snake pit, this den of beasts? Was he in
this hell? Swiftly an automobile whished by. Then a second, a
third. Then, at the Arch of Peace, a tram ground up. Schieppati
looked at the number: it was #1. Wait till it stops. But since
no one got on and no one stepped off, the tram immediately
departed. Having thus exhausted her first excuses, she tried to
invent others. Dully, she began observing the girl who was
swingingly strolling back and forth on the other side of the
street.

But why didn't she do something? Why did she continue to
stay there like that? What was she afraid of? As if in answer
to all these questions, she began walking again. But instead of
crossing Via Pagano, she crossed Via Canova. Now she was
trembling all over and following the slightest movement with
her eyes, there among the shrubs and walks, as if she wanted
to stop everyone in there, pull them close to her, look them
straight in the eye, and question them. Because it wasn't possible that someone shouldn't know him. Her Sandro had too
striking a face. For example, that lock of black hair, who could
forget it? "Here, yes. Try to remember. Not too tall a boy, a
bit squat. Don't be afraid. I'm only his mother. Sandrino.
Sandrino Schieppati. . . ."

Two, three cars. Then, all at once, as if it came from no-
where, a motorcycle passed alongside her, roaring. The two
boys on it shouted ferocious joyous jibes at a group of women
standing in the shadows. Then, still going at full speed, they
yelled back a string of horrible offers and obscene oaths.

And what about the police? Ah, even if they saw her, even

if they stopped her, what could they say? Didn't a mother have the right to go for a walk in the evening looking for her son? And then? "Besides, listen, he's my boy. And that's enough."

That's enough! Yes. But to bestir herself from there, enter into that enclosure where Sandrino, every evening, every night . . . And yet she had to. At least to be able to see them, face to face, those swine! Because they couldn't all be poor, penniless devils, like Luciano. That one in the Boschetti, for instance, that one who had a car with a Como license plate . . . Grab him! Attack him! Tear at him! Shout at him: "Give him back to me! Sandrino is mine!"

It was when one of these fits of grief welled up again that finally she made up her mind. Thus, without knowing how, she found herself on the other side, just where the immense dark pit of those desperate souls began. Up to then she'd seen only women. Women who were strolling along, squalidly, leaving so thick a perfume in their wake as to make one sick—especially she, who at most smelled of soap powder and lye. And if one of them seemed to be working out a deal, then the eyes of all were tense and famished, as if, besides wanting at all costs to see, they wanted at all costs to be seen.

From time to time a car glided among them and rolled to a stop a bit farther on. Muffled rumbling of motors. Metallic screech of the tram. Then, there it was again, that cursed motorcycle returning, coming back right from where it had disappeared before. Once more it tore right alongside her.

But those, those who came to the Park for the same reasons as Sandrino?

Signora Schieppati walked on a few more paces. Finally at the point where the first strip of meadow ended and a smaller road cut off from the wide avenue she saw boys standing. Two of them. Trembling, she watched them awhile. Perhaps she'd come upon someone who knew. Her heart began to pound, her entire head suddenly flushed with heat. But now that she had

60

them there, how could she approach them? Which side should she come from? How should she begin?

With a roar, another motorcycle hurtled past her shoulders. She spun around. Then she began looking again and drawing closer to the two boys, who'd remained standing there, black shadows in the blackness of the night, right at the point where the light of the street lamps died away into nothingness. When she was a few yards away she stopped, trying to hear what the two were saying. Who knows, perhaps a word would slip out, a word that might fill her with hope and faith again. . . .

Instead: "What does she want, that one over there?" one of the two said.

"Oh, another one of those trying to muscle in on our territory," commented the second.

"Beat it," the first said loudly, turning to her and accompanying his words with a gesture. "Beat it."

At first Signora Schieppati wanted to say something or scream. Instead she moved on.

There. Perhaps right at that moment Sandrino was there, behind one of those bushes, whispering, fixing a deal. At any rate, there and only there could she meet, if not him, someone who knew him.

Again she walked on a few steps. Then, convinced that it was better not to go too far off, she stopped. At that instant a car glided around the curve and stopped ahead of the two boys. She heard rather than saw the door squeaking and opening. Then swift as cats the two of them bent down toward the inside of the car. There was a brief conversation, a dry click, a rattling sound cruel and jocund, and off it went.

Now in the gloom only one of the two remained: the taller, thinner one.

Draw near again? the woman asked herself now. Take advantage of the fact that he might be disappointed because he'd been left alone?

"Listen . . ." she said timidly, vaguely waving her hand.

"You speaking to me?" the boy replied.

"To you, yes."

"What do you want?"

"Come here. Here, where there's a little more light and at least we can see each other."

"With all the cops around here tonight?"

Signora Schieppati clutched her bag as if she were clutching her heart.

"Besides, what do you want? Because if you're new here, I tell you right off this is our territory."

The Schieppati didn't have the courage to respond. She remained where she was, motionless, mute, almost as if she were begging for pity.

"Well, are you going to tell me what you're after? Didn't you pass close by me a little while ago? Didn't you?"

"Listen . . . Please, listen . . . Do you happen to know a boy . . ."

"Who?"

"A certain Sandrino."

"Sandrino? Sandrino what?"

"Sandrino, he's about seventeen."

"So?"

"I'm his mother."

Instead of answering, the stranger burst out laughing. Then suddenly he stopped:

"And you come here to look for your son by his real name?" he said. "Around here, names are always changed!"

A moment of silence. Then, flattening himself against a tree trunk:

"Watch out!" the boy cried. "The cops!"

Coldly, cruelly, two headlights jabbed into the bit of meadow where the two stood. Then, as the car turned, the beams turned with them and began scouring around.

"Listen, tonight it's smarter, but I mean smarter, to take off!" the boy said. "Otherwise, we'll both wind up in the clink."

Then, as if gripped by an unexpected feeling of remorse: "Besides," he added, "around here nobody's ever heard about any Sandrino. What do you expect, we meet so many. Good evening, eh? Good evening." And humming, he was swallowed up in the thick swarming gloom of the avenue.

Signora Schieppati remained where she was, motionless, until a train from North Station slid by, whistling, on the right. As if struck by a rifle senselessly fired, two or three sparks shot into the air. And now? Where would she go now? What would she do?

34

Liberata took the last steps hesitantly. When she was just about to cross the vestibule, she looked around to be sure no one was spying. Because when you come right down to it, that's all priests and half-priests like the Olivas were good for: spying.

Once the discussion with Antonio was over, her father and brother had returned to Party headquarters, where another meeting on the organization of the celebration was being held. Therefore, she'd had to stay in the kitchen with her mother, hatching her scheme and waiting for the propitious moment to carry it out. Now, frozen still as she stood against the plaster of the wall, her hands trembled. She felt she wasn't alone any more, but had all the women of the house behind her, and not only of the house but of the entire world, and so she was expressing the anger, the rebellion, the hunger for happiness in all of them.

No matter where she looked, she saw no one. Everything was silent. And except for some breaths of air caressing the bushes and fluttering the flowers, nothing, absolutely nothing stirred. Then she began to creep along close to the wall, and keeping her eyes always toward the garden, she edged two or three yards to the right. As soon as she could feel where the posters were pasted, she attacked with both hands. She felt she was ripping flesh, making the blood spurt. Strip by strip, the posters fell to the ground in scraps.

Having finished one side, she turned to the other. And on that side also, what she was doing and the ripping sound filled her soul with such savage joy that immediately afterward she stooped, scooped up a handful of earth, and began smearing over the scraps of paper that remained stuck to the wall as if she were smearing over the face and flesh of her enemies.

A moment, two. Then, amidst the scraping of her fingers, which were repeating the same act for the fourth, fifth time, she heard a step. She stopped.

"Of course," she muttered to herself. If fate decreed that someone had to see her, better it be one of them. One of that tribe, male or female, who tomorrow would spread it all over the place that she—and she alone—was really responsible for the slashing of the posters. In fact, what she was doing, what else was it but her unparalleled and truly terrible pride?

And that she'd not been mistaken, Liberata Villa realized immediately afterward, when she saw Rina Oliva emerging out of the shadows on the other side of the kitchen gardens. From the oratory hall where she'd gone with a girl friend to see a film, Rina was returning home, but so slowly as to make one think that she did it reluctantly.

Feet set apart, her hands filthy with dirt, scraps of paper, and paste, Liberata Villa watched the girl approaching. Oh, it was just perfect, she said to herself, more than perfect! If anyone existed who ought to see her, this was the one, this little fool who didn't know the difference between one and two. A kind of soft squishy pulp. And now here she is. Here she comes, pale, washed out, without will, without character, without anything. . . .

64

Liberata continued to glare at Rina as if by the fire in her eyes she were trying to bring to white heat the mockery and insults she intended to level against her and, through her, against her entire family of false saints and all those behind them. But with an amazement that took her breath away, she saw the Oliva girl passing by and greeting her with:

"Good evening." And that was all.

Then, taken unawares, Liberata Villa suddenly snatched at the remaining bits of posters still dangling from the wall, tore them off, and squeezing and rolling them up in her hands:

"It should have been a bonfire!" she shouted. "Understand, you ugly little fool! A bonfire! I said a bonfire!"

35

"So you insisted on having your own way this time too, eh?" Signor Schieppati said to his wife as she closed the door behind her. "Well, what did you find out? Come on, speak up."

"Nothing," the woman said.

She was utterly exhausted. What she had seen, the fear that had gripped her at times, those people, those automobiles, those shadows, those encounters! And to think that her Sandrino was among them, lived that kind of life!

"He'll be the end of me, you'll see," she said, approaching the table and dropping her bag on it. "The end . . ."

"Don't worry about it more than he deserves," the husband replied.

"That's easily said, but where is he right now? With all those police patrolling that section. Sooner or later they'll pick him up. They've already made a raid this evening. Rounded up more than twenty of them."

The idea that Sandrino had also been picked up in that raid

was already preying on her mind like a kind of nightmare. The threat of the police, the shame of reformatory and jail—this tormented her even more than her horror at what she could now clearly imagine her son was up to. Three days, three nights—counting tonight, four. Four days, and still no sign of him. Four days during which they knew nothing.

"Perhaps they picked him up yesterday. Anything, now, is possible. . . ."

"Don't get ideas like that in your head, Edvige. If they'd picked him up we would have been told."

After a moment of silence, the husband began to speak again:

"And now, are you convinced it's useless? If they are born wrongheaded, it's best to let them go their own way."

"Their own way," the woman murmured. "Their own way . . ."

Dejected, dead tired, she sat down at the table and took a handkerchief out of her bag; now she was twisting it between her teeth. Then, overcome by a terrible need to pour out her troubles and to weep, she repeated: "Some day or other, he'll be the end of me, you'll see. The end . . ."

"Don't let yourself go like that, Edvige. Maybe tomorrow he'll be home again, sent back by those scoundrels."

"Yes, but then we must take him in hand and make him stop all this, no matter how. Things just can't go on this way!"

Now she was overcome with a feeling of guilt at having caused the quarrel some days ago; why had she not dealt with her son in some other way, more gently, more persuasively?

"Perhaps, instead of scolding him and kicking him out, we ought to get him to understand with kindness. . . ."

"With kindness? But haven't we tried that too? And what came of it?"

"I don't know," the woman said. "I don't know anything any more." Then, overcome again by everything she'd seen and heard in that pit of lost souls: "But why is the world made like that? Why?"

66

Her husband didn't know how to answer. A few minutes went by, then he said he was tired. Sure, tomorrow was Sunday, but he was too sleepy. "My bones ache all over. You come to bed too. In bed it's easier to calm down."

"Calm down? How?"

"Besides, at this point I don't see what else we can do."

"If only I had met one, just one single person willing to tell me something. But not a soul. Nobody. Not a one. They all change their names." Abruptly the woman jerked the handkerchief from between her teeth. Then two big tears trickled down her cheeks. "And there are those who have the gall to say that's how the world must go on! Did you see what they've printed again today on those filthy sheets?" the woman said, as if trying to find the source of her misfortune and the mitigation of her grief in something outside herself. "Have you seen it?"

"Those sheets, God willing, are no longer up."

Another pause. Another long silence. Then the woman, with a voice that seemed to be asking for consolation, any consolation, said:

"And the others? Did you look to see at least whether they were sleeping?"

The husband nodded with a sort of sad growl. Then he repeated his suggestion that she too go to bed.

"No. I can't, the way I feel, Andrea. I'll heat up a little coffee, then, maybe . . ."

Now the husband got up; on his way from the kitchen to his bedroom, he had to cross the room where most of his children were sleeping. A dense, dank smell, almost like that of a barn, assailed him from those beds, and the rattling, irregular sounds of breathing.

"Poor things," he muttered, peering into the gloom. And moved on.

36

"Better, yes! Better she be the one to file charges against me, and tell everybody about it, that sanctimonious little sap!"

Having waited in vain for her father and brother to come back, Liberata decided to follow her mother's example, shutting herself up in her room. That is, if one could call a room that hole obtained partly out of the hallway and partly by narrowing the space where her mother and father slept on one side and her brothers on the other. A hole in which day bed, chair, hangers, and night table could scarcely fit, so that she had to keep all her clothes and linen in her parents' wardrobe.

She was quite aware of what people said about Rina: that she was the only member of the Oliva family who didn't share their nastiness and fanaticism. But a servant of the priests she remained all the same, so that the places she frequented were always places where priests were to be found. So deeply emotional had been that silent colloquy between them a little while earlier that even now Liberata seemed to be reliving it. Despite the fact that the outcome had turned out very differently from what she had foreseen.

No reproach, not a glance. Instead, "Good Evening." Did she want to overwhelm her, perhaps, with that famous charity about which they never stopped talking? But if she had intended to set her an example with those fine manners, she was mistaken and plenty mistaken! Besides, all her fine manners and all her charity would end up in her filing charges, all the same, just to keep in style with her family. Liberata had no doubts about that. Rina would point her finger at her in front of everyone, and opening her mouth begin to shout: "She was the one! I saw her myself, while I was returning from the nuns. I saw her with my own eyes!" And afterward, the nuns, like the others, in one of those big rooms where all the sodality ladies of the neighborhood met every Saturday evening and Sunday, would be saying to her over and over: "Good girl, good girl . . ."

"Good girl, shit!" Liberata muttered at that point. Then she tried to change position, get more comfortable, and fall asleep in the narrow cot.

37

When he got out of the big shot's car and came home, neither his father nor brother had returned. The kitchen was quiet. And even from his sister's den, not a sound, not a stir.

"Thank goodness for that," Antonio said to himself. At least tonight there wouldn't be the argument he had expected. Which didn't mean it would never take place. Simply that it was postponed. However, weary as he felt, even that seemed a gift. Reassured by this, Antonio began to open the small valise and take out the dirty clothes which tomorrow he would give his mother to wash.

The snap of the lock. The damp shine of his shorts. The boxing gloves rolling as he put them on the table . . .

It was the violence rather than the suddenness of her action that made him turn about. The door, unexpectedly opening, revealed his sister against the darkness of the bedroom. She was staring at him with a hard pitiless expression as if she wanted to pass judgment on him. Antonio tried to free himself of that stare by staring back. But Liberata stared him down, saying:

"Not even if those were love letters . . ."

"What? These?" the young man asked, lifting up his shorts from the table.

"Those and all the rest."

"One does what one can," Antonio replied, trying to be as casual as possible about the matter.

"Also by saying No?"

"What do you mean, saying No?"

"Saying No! The No you threw in everybody's face tonight!"

"That way too. After all, I was the one who signed the contract."

"You make me sick! You don't even seem to belong to our breed any more!"

"Why? What breed do we belong to?"

"The breed that never gives up."

"You?" Antonio said looking at his sister with a kind of livid joy. "Don't make me talk, please. Better we keep quiet. Better for both of us."

"Quiet, me? To keep me quiet, remember, they've got to sew up my mouth! And certainly you won't be the one to do it, with all your false notions about boxing and glory!"

"Stop getting excited! Stop yelling!" Antonio replied. "By now you ought to know very well that as far as I'm concerned, you can talk from morning till night, if you don't get on my nerves first. In fact, you can go out into the piazza and hold a meeting if you like. As if it isn't well known that the only thing you're missing is this," he added, dropping his hand on the shorts.

"What this?" Liberata cried.

"Balls! That's what you need. Balls!"

With one leap Liberata hurled herself upon her brother, fixing him with the eyes of a wounded beast.

"And I really don't understand why, instead of worrying so much about membership cards, and the headquarters and the Party, they haven't thought about finding someone to give you a screwing. As if that weren't also an obligation!"

"Antonio!" Liberata screamed. "I'll find someone to give me a screwing myself, if I want to! And without anybody's help!

70

But as long as men are like your president and his pretty pals . . ."

"Why? What's so strange about my president and his pals?"

"They've got . . ."

"What have they got?"

For an instant, Liberata's devastated eyes glared straight into her brother's, then she said:

"Money! That's what they've got. And since they're stuffed with it, they don't give a damn about us, they think they've got the right to change everything. Even what should never be changed. Money! And you and your kind let yourselves be bought! You disgust me! Disgust me!"

"I?" Antonio replied. "As far as I'm concerned, Morini can do as he likes. Besides, I've never seen such beautiful women as you find around him. Certainly, if I waited till I saw them up there at Party headquarters . . ."

"Beautiful? Beautiful, because he's got a full wallet. Beautiful because his father also sold out on what was once his life and began acting like a swine and a thief. And when it comes to beauty, if I've got to say it all out, I don't think your big shot only has women. Binda, for instance. What do you think, people don't know about it? And he's not the only one. Those perverts are corrupting everybody. Sandrino, look at Sandrino. Four days, four, he hasn't been seen."

"What's that got to do with me?"

"Plenty! Because you too are selling out to their money and their ideas! Beautiful women! As if beauty were everything!"

"Well, at least it's something! Besides, that's the way I see it. As far as I'm concerned, I don't give a hoot for political parties, workers, and all the rest of it. You live only once and I mean to enjoy it as much as possible."

"Even at the price of trampling all over the hearts of your own people and your own conscience?"

"But who's trampling on anything? I let everyone do as they please. If you want to know, from Monday on I don't even have to set foot in the factory. Just think a bit whether people like Morini are of any use to me. . . ."

Liberata remained silent for a moment.

"Think and do as you wish," she said. "Enough for tonight. Your brother and father will tell you the rest."

"The rest? I'm going to sleep now," Antonio replied. "I've got to get some sleep just like you and them, no more, no less. And if they want to make a big fuss, all right, then let's have that one as well. After all, in this dump here we're used to arguments for quite a while now!"

With a click, Antonio shut the valise, put on the chair all the laundry he meant to give his mother tomorrow, and left the kitchen. Liberata remained standing there for a few moments as if the talk with her brother had made her face herself naked and defenseless. Then she too withdrew into her room.

38

A livid dawn, as if time had turned back two or three months. Livid, cold, whipped by a wind that made you think: God knows how much snow there must be on the mountains!

It was barely six when Signora Oliva opened the kitchen window. The sudden change would have startled her had she not been prepared for it. For her father-in-law had lamented all night and immediately found reasons for his complaints: "It's the weather. It's going to change. Either it rains tomorrow, or it'll be even worse."

"What a character!" the woman said to herself, closing the windows. "He predicts everything." Although Mass would not start yet for a half hour, she wanted to go to confession, and so decided to get to church ahead of time. So, after having brought the coffee to her father-in-law and her husband, she left the house, keeping the old man's advice well in mind. "See what's happened," he'd said, "and if they've ripped it off, come up and tell me, but come back right away."

Thus, in the leaden gray of the hour rendered more ominous rather than relieved by the light of the street lamps, Signora Oliva was the first to see the havoc that had been done to the posters that night as well.

"Will they never stop, those wretches!" she said, stiffening all over. Then, turning back and racing up the stairs again: "But why must we put up with it? Why don't we get rid of them? What is that gang down in Rome doing about it?"

Her swift nervous steps resounded in the stair well and managed to awaken Redenta, who was still making use of the few miserable hours of sleep left from the night. Then, abruptly flinging the door wide open, Signora Oliva cried:

"They're swine! That's what they are!"

With a fling of his hand, the old man pulled the blanket off his face.

"Why?" he asked in his usual voice.

"They've torn them off again," Enrica replied, passing from the kitchen into the bedroom.

"What!" the old man exclaimed.

"They haven't left a single piece whole! And what remains is smeared over with crap."

"You see?" the grandfather cried, his excitement stirred with anger, joy, and indignation. "Luigi, I'm talking to you."

Then the grandson, who hadn't yet managed to wake up entirely, turned his eyes toward the old man. Meanwhile, from the other room, the father was asking for more specific details.

"There you are! And all of you in church, instead of staying down there to watch what they were up to, as I said. In church listening to Don Rinaldo! File charges! Now I hope you understand! File charges that will get rid of them once and for all!"

Only then did Rina begin tossing back and forth in her bed and understand what was happening.

73

39

What gnawed at Liberata's soul day after day during the whole week was the way young Rina Oliva behaved. Why hadn't she said anything? Why did she keep silent in front of her relatives, her father, mother, and brother who were trying to accuse the Villas, and silent in front of those who were inviting her to prove that she had seen them in the act of tearing off the posters? They'd even had an official inquiry. Late Sunday afternoon, the carabinieri had come, called by the Oliva family and other members of the Christian Democratic Party. But even in front of them, the girl hadn't spoken.

"Try to remember, Rina," her mother had asked her. "When you returned from the oratory, didn't you see whether they were still there?"

"My mind was on other things."

"On other things, on other things! And you knew what catching them red-handed meant to us."

"Sure," Liberata had interjected, "and if your sweet little saint found them all ripped up when she came back what would that prove?"

"It would prove," Signora Oliva had quickly replied, "that you'd already been down there at that hour, you and the rest of your precious family!"

"Because according to you they've got nothing else to do but waste time down in the courtyard over a couple of lousy posters?"

"If ours are lousy, yours are lousy too!"

Wishing to calm things down and not get involved in a mess which, basically, didn't seem worth all the fuss, the brigadier tried to make both sides promise him that there would be no more fights or discussions on that subject. Except that just when his effort seemed on the point of succeeding, Signora Oliva's grumbling stung Liberata once more into action:

"All right, then, say it!" she shouted, grabbing Rina's arm. "Go on, say it, since your mother never wants to take anybody's word, and keeps thinking it was me! Go ahead, say it! Did you see me? Speak up! Did you see me?"

Rina hesitated a moment, then said:

"No. I didn't see anything."

Nothing, eh? Really nothing! But why? What was she up to? What self-interest was she concealing behind that continuous stubborn No? All week long Liberata had been putting these questions to herself over and over again: on the job when the click-click of the machines in the ready-to-wear department where she worked let up a bit; in the evening at home when she was resting, if it could be called rest. Until, unable to find any explanation herself, she decided to speak to Redenta about it.

"Listen," she said to her one Friday evening as soon as she set foot in the Project after having left the plant, "I've got to talk to you about something." And she told her.

"What do you make of it?"

"Me? I don't know. . . ."

"But does it seem possible to you that, having seen me, but really seen me . . ."

"What do you want, my dear Liberata, nowadays anything is possible."

"Yes, but why? That's what I keep asking myself: Why?"

However, not even Redenta, who seemed to know everything about everyone, had managed to find an answer. As to being different from the other members of the Oliva family, oh, Rina was certainly different: shy, reserved, kind. "For example," Redenta said, "I've always asked myself: Who knows whether she really shares her family's ideas!" Now Liberata agreed: different, shy, reserved, kind, who knows whether she really shared her family's ideas, etc., etc. But from that to the point of boycotting her family's principles—as she'd obviously done —there was a mighty big difference.

Speak about it at home? Perhaps Carlo would have the answer? But Liberata didn't dare to say anything to anyone: neither to her mother, nor her father, nor even to her brother.

Thus, when that Sunday at five there happened what did happen at Party headquarters, the first flash crossing Liberata's mind was:

"She's behind it! Since it's clear someone had to do it, that bitch has been spying all along! With that half-martyred air of hers, she wouldn't have got enough satisfaction turning just me in! It would have created a scandal and ruined her bigger plans."

And amidst the fury that more or less swept everyone in the hall, while the police, without too much consideration, were hustling them all out, Liberata tugged at her brother's jacket, drew him aside, and said:

"It's obvious that it was those swine. But if you want to know exactly, you know who? Rina. That hypocrite!"

Gripped by emotion, Carlo didn't reply. As he listened to his sister explaining all her reasons for her suspicion, he began saying to himself that this time they'd pay for it, and pay for it in what they held dearest.

40

What had happened at Party headquarters that afternoon was this: right in the middle of the celebration, the inspector of the Society for Authors' Rights, accompanied by four detectives, presented himself and without much ceremony requested the permit from the man in charge.

"But this isn't a performance," the man in charge replied, without raising his voice. "This is a party."

"A family party," Carlo explained, also trying to keep his voice down so that none of the people present should realize anything was happening.

"Ah, yes, and those there, what are they doing?" the inspector replied, pointing to a kind of stage set up for the occasion, where at that moment the tiny orchestra and two comics were just beginning their comedy act.

"That's just to make everybody laugh."

"Is that so? Now listen here, you better come along. You better come along if you don't want everything just strung up by the heels here."

And then they'd suspended everything, if not by the heels. The inspector had known that tickets had been sold for admission. That was enough to transform the party into a performance, even though, according to its organizers, it was supposed to remain just a party. Naturally, someone must have been spying in order to let the Society for Authors' Rights know about it. Nor was it difficult to discover who it was: the Christian Democratic Party and its affiliates. But who had it been, precisely, in flesh and blood?

A string of imprecations had run through the hall, mumbled, however, in low tones, since the agents had decided not to leave the place until all the participants were out. In fact, as a memento, they'd even left two small trucks outside which were still keeping vigil at the building entrance. The building was a big shed which up until 1943 had served as a gymnasium, meeting place, and exhibition hall for the Italian Fascist Youth organization.

News of this abuse of power spread swiftly through the area. And it also came to the Project immediately, borne by the Villa girl running headlong as if she were out of her mind.

"Those bastards!" she shouted as soon as she was in view of the house. "They've done it again!"

"What!"

"Again! Again! Now we've got to wipe them all out!"

"What have they done?"

"They've broken up the meeting," Liberata explained. "They've taken the cashbox, and what's more, they're going to make us pay a fine! And you want to know who the spy was? That one there!" she shouted pointing up at the Oliva kitchen on the top floor of the house.

It was five o'clock. Via Aldini was full of strollers. Some motorcycles and scooters were roaring across it or racing around, weaving strange patterns. Among groups and couples strolling back and forth, there were many who stopped to hear what had happened. In a short while the crowd grew so large that in order to get by, a car had to stop and blow its horn five or six times. Then, when it succeeded in breaking through the traffic jam, an endless stream of abuse was hurled from the crowd against those inside:

"Thieves!"

"Pigs!"

"The street is also for poor people!"

"They act like bosses! Just because they've got four wheels under them!"

"Yes, and if things are allowed to go on as they are," Liberata broke in, arrogantly, "in a little while they'll be using automobiles just to murder us!"

After this final piece of abuse, the discussion resumed, dominated always by Liberata Villa's voice, which could be heard above all the others. And when someone hazarded the shadow of a doubt concerning her assurance about the spy's identity, Liberata cried:

"I beg your pardon! What do you mean, it must be someone more important! Besides, more important, less important, that's still where all the ruination comes from. We're the fools, keeping those murderers here, in our house! We ought to make life impossible for that gang up there! That's what we should do!"

"I'm afraid it's they who'll make life impossible for us," Signora Ruschetti said.

"Sure," Liberata Villa replied. "So long as everyone does the same as you, spending their Sundays here gossiping instead of coming to the headquarters . . ."

"But I've never understood a thing about politics."

"There you are! But you've got to understand it," Liberata cried. "Understand it and also become involved in it. Otherwise, we'll just be thrown on the dump by them! All of us! Us, our sons, our children, our brothers, and our husbands! Can't you see? Our children, our brothers, and our husbands!" The desperation with which she shouted and repeated the last word, as if she wanted to take possession of a blessing that she lacked, cast a shadow of dismay among all the listening women. There was a new silence. Then the discussion was started up again by Signora Moroni and continued more furiously and angrily than before.

41

When Carlo came in sight of the house, it was already past seven.

Although he was limp as a rag as a result of all the preparatory work, and then his anger and dread afterward, now he stepped forward decisively as if poison rather than blood ran in his veins. Tonight he was overwhelmed, conquered, by hatred, a feeling that had scarcely touched him before. Now he felt and lived in the blazing force and violence of hatred.

It wasn't enough that his brother's behavior had shamed him in front of everyone. No: he also had to put up with this other offense, this other greater humiliation as well. "And then they go on talking about freedom!" he muttered. "But what freedom is there for us except surrendering to their ideas and their markets and becoming their servants and their slaves?"

He continued to walk, and with each step his face grew paler. He clenched his fists and ground his teeth, and a cold sweat began to break out all over his body.

To rebel, to hate, and then to strike. It didn't matter whom. Provided it was someone and something of theirs. Their ideas had taken flesh and blood; therefore, he would plunge his knife into them with fuller joy, knowing that afterward he might trample upon them and spit on them.

In such a mood, Carlo reached the garden. Probably, of himself, he would not have been aware of anything had not the intensity with which he felt himself being stared at made him turn around at a certain moment. Then, with a kind of terror, he saw young Rina Oliva standing there at the right of the hedge, staring at him as if she had been waiting for him. Abruptly, the boy stopped stock-still, trying with equal abruptness to regain the offensive by returning that glance with one intended to insult the girl. But Rina did not change expression, not even by a shade.

Carlo felt a twinge of indecision. Then, as if he no longer understood anything, he hid his head in his hands. When he began walking again, he didn't even try to see whether Rina was still there. He only managed to notice that then, as always, Redenta was sitting quietly at her window, her eyes peering down, spying.

"Doesn't she have anything better to do, that gossip?" he said to himself, and entered the house.

42

A dismal oppressive silence hung over the kitchen. Even if the stream of abuse and curses hadn't been sufficient to get it out of their systems, everyone was worn out and had lost the desire to start all over again and continue. Besides, why start all over again and continue? What was the use? None whatever. By now it was clear. They had the knife by the handle. And the spying, the celebration that had been ruined, the charges that were sure to follow, were all evidence in the face of which it was no longer possible to have any illusions.

The mother was the first to say anything, as soon as Carlo set foot in the house.

"Well, what did you find out?" she asked, rather wearily.

"Nothing," Carlo replied.

Thus, that attempt to break the silence also failed. Swiftly, furiously, Carlo went to the sink, turned on the faucets, and began to wash.

"Sons of bitches!" Liberata muttered between her teeth.

Another long silence. Then, seeing that her daughter showed no signs of changing her monotonous grumbling, the mother said:

"A lot you accomplish, talking like that!"

"A lot more," Carlo interrupted while washing, "than playing the he-man with underwear and boxing gloves."

The reference to Antonio fell flat. But Carlo, his temper rising, picked it up again at once:

"And if you really care to know what I think, he'd probably have the gall to burst out laughing if he knew about it."

"Now don't exaggerate, Carlo," the mother said. "So long as you talk about his not caring, his indifference, maybe, but this . . ."

"When you begin with indifference, you can very well end up as a spy. Spying's worse."

81

"Carlo!" the father shouted, raising his head from the news-paper.

Carlo didn't reply. He put the towel back in its place, then stood by the window, looking out.

"I'd like to hope," said the father after a while, "that it was just nerves made you say that about spying."

"Nerves?" Carlo said. "Why? We can expect anything from certain traitors. You know that very well."

"But Carlo," the mother interjected, "do you know what you're saying?"

Instead of answering, Carlo shrugged his shoulders and continued staring down into the courtyard.

"Do you know?" the mother repeated.

"He knows," Liberata said, "and he has all the good reasons in the world to know."

After this little altercation, the kitchen was pervaded again by a silence gloomier and heavier than before.

Carlo continued standing at the window. When he finally decided to turn around, he murmured: "If I had him here, right now, I'd choke him. . . ."

"Who?" the mother cried.

"Who? Him, your pet!"

"But what's he got to do with all this business?"

"He or someone else, what do I care?"

As he broke away from the window, Carlo's furious glance had frightened his sister, on whom his blazing eyes had fallen more piercingly than on the others.

The father waited a moment, then introduced a note of calmness:

"You young ones are a bunch of hysterics!" he said. "What's needed in life is courage, faith, and patience. Not explosions, anger, and abuse! You have to know how to bide your time, you have to know how to suffer. . . ."

"And what's the use?"

"The use is that you have to learn that these aren't battles to be won overnight. If we had acted like you when Mussolini was running the show here, we would have left behind us nothing but tombs, bloodshed, and disasters."

In saying these words, a sadness past consolation suffused the old man's soul, as if he had suddenly drawn upon himself the entire past, with all its hardships, its grief, and its suffering, and now was overwhelmed by it. At that moment, the one who felt closest to him was his wife, she who hadn't hesitated to marry him although it meant abandoning the family in which she'd been born and the ideas with which she'd been brought up.

"And besides," the father said after a pause, "who ever managed to accomplish anything without trouble."

"They!" Carlo shouted.

"Yes, but what have they accomplished?"

"It doesn't matter what they've accomplished. What matters is that they order us around, everybody orders us around!" A pause, then again: "But don't kid yourselves that things can end up the same way this time too."

Now Carlo had begun to tremble.

"Carlo?" the mother exclaimed. "What's the matter with you now? Calm down. Listen to me, calm down. Sit here, sit down here a moment."

"Sit down, me?" Carlo replied. "Why? Why am I trembling? But you ought to know very well that if I've been brought to this, it's their fault, *their* fault!"

Then, still trembling, he walked toward the window and once more gazed toward the hedge with a knifelike glance.

In the kitchen there was another long silence. Then, while his sister started grumbling again:

"Look," Carlo said, "while you're getting ready, I'm going down. Because staying here tonight gives me a splitting headache." And without looking at anyone, not even at Liberata who was still nervously and closely watching her brother's least movements, he left the kitchen and went downstairs.

43

It had come to him like a flash. All at once it crossed his mind and at once destroyed any hesitancy. It was right; in fact, more than right. And nothing, absolutely nothing, would be more likely to calm him down.

The suspicion that Liberata might be watching from the kitchen hardly disturbed him at all. More likely, Redenta would be watching. But once in the garden, a single glance upward was enough to assure him that fortunately Redenta had left her post at the windowsill. He crossed the court. Then as he reached the end of the hedge he began glancing at the Oliva girl with an expression of hatred and scorn, ferocity and fear.

"All I need is for her to understand," he said to himself. "Understand, and come up to me."

Again he took two or three steps to the left. Then he walked slowly along the part opposite the hedge, and when he reached the point where a group of elderberry bushes seemed to guard him against anyone looking from the house, he stopped.

Because of the hour no one was about. Nevertheless, Carlo glanced about two or three times. Only when he was quite sure did he plunge his hands into his pockets and begin glancing at Rina again.

This colloquy of looks lasted several minutes. Rina had turned white and begun to tremble; but she was no less sweet for all her agitation. And this only intensified Carlo's need to carry out his sudden desperate plan. Thus, when at last the girl heeded his signal and began to move he opened his fists against his thighs. Then, tightening them again, he said to himself: "Now, she understands. Now I can do as I want." He waited till the girl came within two or three yards of him. Aware that she was still hesitant, he started speaking.

"I've got to see you."

"See me?" Rina replied.

"See you, yes, but alone."

"When?"

"Tonight." And since the girl showed no sign of replying:

"I said tonight. After dinner."

Rina lowered her eyes. Again Carlo glanced at her as if he were striking her with a paw. Then almost as if he couldn't really believe that he was about to realize his plan, he added:

"You can always tell your family that you had to go see some priest or nun. . . ."

"But where?" Rina asked after a little while, hardly raising her head. "It's not possible here."

"Who said anything about here?" With each word Carlo's eyes flared more brightly. "We can see each other at the highway, near the bridge."

"The Sanatorium bridge?"

"Yes, there."

"What time?"

"At nine."

For a moment Rina looked at Carlo. Then she lowered her head and blushed.

"I'll be there at nine," she said. Once more, and for a longer interval, she looked at Carlo Villa. "But you'll be there too, won't you?" she added.

And, joy and fear gripping her heart, she turned about to retrace her steps and re-enter the house.

44

"Ah, that must be him," Signora Schieppati said, as soon as she recognized her son's steps coming up the staircase. Except for

Sandrino, who hadn't come home now for days and days, everyone was at table. Only Vittorio was missing and it was precisely he whom she was waiting for.

"The next time, try to get back earlier," the father said, when the boy had opened the door and entered. "And don't try to tell us a cock-and-bull story about the game, eh?"

"Actually . . ." Vittorio said.

"Actually what?" the father replied.

"I haven't been at the sports field all this time."

"And if not at the field, where?"

The mother, not unaware of the difficulty in which her son might find himself, drew close to him and said:

"All right, all right, now sit down. Go, sit down. Then we'll talk about it, if we have to."

"No, I prefer to talk now," Vittorio said, suddenly feeling hot.

"Well, talk, then," the father ordered.

The boy glanced into his father's face, then, for a longer time, into his mother's. Finally, he said:

"I saw Sandrino. . . ."

"Sandrino? Where? Speak up. Where?"

"He came to the sports field. It was just before the game ended. . . ."

"And you couldn't get him to come home?"

"How could I? If he didn't want me to talk about that?"

"Oh, he didn't, eh? You see, you?" Schieppati said, turning to his wife. "You see whether it's worth while, getting so upset over that scoundrel?"

"What did he tell you?" the woman burst out, ignoring her husband's remark.

"Nothing! He asked me how you all were, we spoke a little about the team, we went to the bar for a coke. . . ."

"And then?"

Vittorio, who had begun to dip his spoon in his soup dish, lowered his head and kept silent.

86

"Then?" the father insisted. "I said, then what! Speak up!"

Now all the four other children had stopped eating and, with frightened expressions, were looking at their brother.

"Well, Vittorio," the mother said, entering into the discussion as gently as possible. "You wouldn't . . . Vittorio? Say something, Vittorio!"

At that very moment, the next to the youngest child sneezed, and that unexpected sudden noise seemed to break the spell. Then, while the little ones began giggling because of what had come out of the nose and ended in the plate, Vittorio drew a five-thousand-lire note from his pocket and handed it to his mother.

"He gave me this," he said and lowered his head again.

The mother took the note, looked at her husband for an instant, then with a swift determined gesture tore it to pieces.

"And now go wash up, because this money is evil. Understand? Evil!"

The children stopped laughing. From where he sat, the father seemed to be asking the woman why she had done what she had done: in their state of affairs five thousand lire wasn't a joke. However, instead of talking about the subject again, he simply said to his children:

"Eat, eat, go ahead and eat, or we'll never get done here tonight."

And while Vittorio, who had hastened to the sink to do as his mother bade him, now returned to his place, the sounds of soup spoons once more scooping up the minestra and chunks of bread could be heard in the kitchen.

45

Triumph and celebration pervaded the Oliva household. During the entire meal they'd done nothing but speak about "justice," "sooner or later you've got to pay," and "at long last." That was it: to ignore the law, as that bunch had done, was a crime. When they, on the other hand, organized a show at the oratory, or at the Christian Democratic headquarters, they never even dreamed of trying to avoid paying taxes. In fact, taxes had to be paid, and scrupulously, otherwise how could a government survive and go ahead? That afternoon's happening showed —and showed better than any words—that it was useless to get all wrought up about personal revenge: life itself always took care of settling debts. So, for a while, at least for a little while, those damned Communists would keep their mouths shut.

"You think so?" Enrica said at that point.

"Well, they won't want to run the risk of jail again," her husband replied.

"Nonsense! You can expect anything of those atheists. They're so filled with venom . . ."

"In any case, they've already got a good lesson. And all their revolutionary partners with them."

The enthusiasm was such that Rina succeeded more easily than she had expected in sticking to her lie about a film she wanted to see with a girl friend at the oratory.

The only one who showed that he wasn't fully satisfied, despite everybody else's obvious contentment, was the grandfather. Aside from the fact that for him the only solution would have been jail, his discontent derived from a realization that basically this was only an episode. "How important is this, if you think how big just Italy is, not to mention the world?" In short, the same severity had to be applied everywhere, but everywhere, and seriously. They shouldn't be left even an inch of free ground, those atheists! "Instead, look what they cook up! All you have to do is open any one of their papers and read the headlines. Sacrilege, lies, destructiveness, hatred, envy, and there you are! And then when they seem to be defending the people's interests, it's only to make fools of those poor idiots standing there listening to them. And they swallow it! Like all of them here in this barracks. Idiots, sure, but idiots baptized in hell."

46

For ten minutes now Rina had been waiting, hidden behind a bush, just where the ground sloped toward the edge of the highway. Between fear and terror she watched the cars approaching from the other side of the bridge, crossing, and immediately racing on toward Novate, Cinisello, and Sesto. Each of them exploded a fan of light into her face, then with a roar disappeared into the darkness. For a few moments she could see the red taillight growing smaller and smaller, then nothing.

She didn't even know, herself, whether her fear was due to the lie with which she'd concealed her appointment from her family, or whether it was a result of not knowing how Carlo would behave toward her. She only knew that she was afraid. And while she had realized almost at once that, buried as she was in the grass, leaves, and branches, she needn't worry about being observed by any of the crowd crossing the bridge, the real problem, she knew, would be to recognize among so many people the one she was waiting for. In fact, she hoped that she would hear Carlo even before seeing him. That hard, nervous, and yet rolling gait as if just to bestir himself took so much out of him! That step of his which she had learned for many months now to distinguish, and to distinguish without anyone being the wiser.

Three, four cars. A new, long silence. Then, on the bridge,

two motorcycles that seemed to be chasing each other. Singing, shouts, curses. Rina heard the exhausts roaring over her head while from above headlights fell flush upon her for an instant, cruelly.

Now, from where she was standing, she could see all of Vialba. The massive outlines of the houses, the numberless threads of light from windows and staircases. Farther to the right some trams squeaking and struggling, before heading down toward the last stop of the line at the Sanatorium. Then, if she turned her eyes still farther north, there was the Pero gas flame, stinking less than usual tonight.

A truck on the Milano-Bergamo run. Then, from the meadow's edge at the sports field, a dog barking. Then a rustling, like steps; they were coming from the edge of the highway right near her. Two lovers, she thought, even before seeing them. And she wasn't wrong. Luckily, however, both of them were swallowed up almost immediately at the same spot from which they had emerged only a moment before. Now again she began to look down the highway. Carlo was late, really too late. Who knows? Perhaps he'd intended to offend her by making an appointment that he had no intention of keeping. But why? Why? Carlo, the Carlo she'd always imagined, couldn't do such a thing. Despite everything they were saying, despite the Party, despite his ideas . . .

And in fact here he was. At the sight of him Rina clapped her hand over her mouth, not to cry out. Then watching Carlo approach, she began to tremble as if she herself didn't know what she was looking at; but now she was trembling with a joy that set her whole being athrob.

It took two or three minutes for Carlo to reach the head of the bridge. When he got there he peered down for a moment, then he said:

"Ah, there you are," and immediately crossed the four or five yards of escarpment leading to the hedge.

Now they were together at last, face to face. They stared at

90

each other a moment without even shaking hands. Only Rina smiled faintly. But just at that instant a car rounding the curve thrust the cold icy beam of its headlights upon them.

"And now," Carlo said, "where do we go?"

"Wherever you want to," Rina replied. "I don't know much about these things, I . . ."

"Oh, sure! You only know about nuns, priests, and altars!" Carlo commented with a coarse laugh. But the laughter stuck in his throat. "Come on, this way. We'll follow the embankment, turn left . . ."

"I'm afraid there's someone there," Rina ventured.

"So what? Besides, what do you think they're doing? Whoring, whoring, like us. Because I hope you understand. I've only made you come here for that."

Rina said nothing.

"Well, you ready?" Carlo said. He'd already begun to move, then all at once he spun around and pinched Rina on the chin. "Just don't start bawling for the Madonna," he added. Then, setting out again: "Come on! Come on! I like to get these things over with in a hurry!"

Step for step, Rina followed Carlo along the entire embankment, which, at the end, also swerved where the Sanatorium wood gave onto the meadows and first garden plots.

"More comfortable here!" Carlo said, stopping and looking around.

Although she felt strangely happy, Rina continued to tremble.

"What's the matter? You afraid? Of what? You don't have to worry. Nobody'll see us here, not even your Jesus Christ. Because I . . ." Carlo said, all at once seizing her around the waist and drawing her close to him. "I . . . I . . . hate you. Understand? I hate you! Like all the rest of your tribe! A disgusting lot!" he shouted. "Killers! Bloodsuckers who live off our backs! I said bloodsuckers, understand?"

Rina had allowed herself to be tightly clasped and shaken. Now she glanced at Carlo for a moment and said:

"But Carlo, Carlo darling?"

"Carlo darling my foot! Down! Get down on the ground," Villa said, thrusting her at his feet. "And here's the newspaper too," he added, pulling a copy of *Unità,* all folded and refolded, out of his pocket. "Otherwise, your family will notice all the dirt and muck sticking to you. But even if they do, who cares? So much the better! Because I don't want anything but this. And if you're kidding yourself that you can please me even once, you're wrong. Because you disgust me! Disgust me!" he repeated.

Rina, who had remained on the ground, instead of bursting out crying, got to her knees for a moment and tried to put her arms around Carlo's legs.

"Let go of me! If anybody's going to do any squeezing around here it's me!"

"Carlo . . ." Rina said, "Carlo . . ." she repeated. Then, since Carlo seemed to hesitate: "Carlo, you're trembling. . . ."

"And you, what do you think you're doing? Don't you see where you are! Down there where I've kicked you like a bitch!" Carlo said, staring at her from above. "But where's all your holiness, tell me, if soon as someone whistles, you come running like all the others? Where is it? Tell me. I said tell me, where is it?"

"But I love you, Carlo. . . ."

"Love me! Love! That's how they all start! Sure, you couldn't get it put in by calling on the Holy Virgin!"

There was a moment of silence in the meadow. Only the rumbling of two cars could be heard; their lights faded away, skimming like huge wings across the grass. Then Rina turned to cling to Carlo's legs. But now her entire body imprisoned him, and with such force that Carlo could not break loose.

"I said that I love you, Carlo. Compared with that, nothing matters to me. And it's not only since tonight that I've been in love with you. I don't even know when I began to love you. But I'm ready to do anything for you. . . ."

92

"What did you say?" Carlo said without moving.

"I said, anything whatever. . . ."

"Even to turn against your family?"

Rina hesitated a moment, then she said:

"And haven't I done it?"

"Well, then you're nothing but a whore, you too! In fact, worse! Worse, because you cover yourself with the Mass, prayers, and holy water! But underneath"—and with a brusque movement, Carlo freed himself from the girl, bent over her, and held her there, a few inches away—"underneath you're even more disgusting than those in the houses. So how do you expect to be treated?"

A moment of hesitation. Then, still more furiously:

"Do you know what French kissing means? Yes? And you know how to do it as well as you know how to play the part of a spy? Because who turned us in, tell me, who was it, if not you, or someone from your house? And now just look what's done with saints like you. Here, do you know what this is?" Carlo said, taking Rina's hand. "Feel it? Speak! Don't stand there like an idiot! Because I've made you come here only to insult you, offend you, dirty you. Understand? And the more whorishness we do, the more pleased I'll be. Well, can we begin?" he said, drawing his mouth close to Rina's but then suddenly stopping as if he really first wanted to have her approval.

As soon as she felt Carlo's lips drawing close to hers, Rina murmured two or three times:

"Carlo, Carlo darling . . ."

Then she lifted her hands up along the boy's back and, pressing with desperate sweetness against the woolen sweater, she began to caress him and draw him down upon her. "Come here. Like that . . . dearest Carlo. Do you know how happy I am to be here tonight with you? Oh, Carlo. . . . Carlo darling."

47

To sleep, yes, but how, if just when he was about to start insulting her all over again and shout that she was more rotten than any of the others he'd been with up to then, and that he'd made her come here only in order to pour out on some member of her party all the hatred he'd stored up for so many years against her bosses, her priests, and her Masses ("because you've also ruined my brother. You know Antonio? Yes, him. You've dragged him over to your side. And I want you to know that if I've come here tonight just to get laid with a poor sap like you, it's only so's I can tell everybody that I was the one to break your cherry. Me, get it? Whore of a whore!")—how, if, the more he had clasped her and the more he had shouted at her, the more he had realized that what he was clasping and against whom he was shouting was something that set him trembling and made what he was doing and saying seem disturbing at first, then horrible, and finally almost like murder?

"Oh, if you only knew how happy I am, dearest Carlo. . . ."

And the more he bit her, the more he covered her with spit, the more he said that everything he was doing he was doing only out of contempt, the more she murmured:

"But I love you, Carlo. I love you. Who do you think I pray for when I go to church? For you, for me. So we could be like this forever, like tonight. . . ."

"Ah, like this forever? Like tonight forever, eh? But you'll never be like this with me again, never again. I've done it just to get it out of my system! Just because I had to, understand? Had to insult you, dirty you, fill you up with it like any old bitch. And you can thank your Jesus Christ if I haven't strangled you, because I felt, if you really want to know, I felt like . . ."

At this point, instead of drawing away, Rina stroked his head and said:

94

"If you really have to . . ."

"What?"

"If you really have to . . . For me, you're the only one in the world and if it's not you it won't be anybody."

"But your priests? Your nuns? What'll they say when they know that you've been here getting yourself licked all over by someone out of hell?"

"You're not out of hell, Carletto. You're from the Project, like me, like your Antonio, like your Liberata. . . ."

"What will they say?" he cried again, trying to overcome his weakness, feeling himself about to succumb. "What will they do? They'll kick you out of their churches, their oratories, even out of their house. Isn't that so? Speak!"

Then Rina had clung even more tenderly to him, saying:

"I'm ready for that too, if it means staying with you."

"Well, you better get any such idea right out of your head. Because you're not going to stay with me. Never. Understand? And now let go of me. Don't think I'm going to give you a good time all night. Let go of me, I said, you whore!"

All at once he was on his feet looking down at her stretched out there on the grass, on the crumpled newspaper, her skirt in disorder, her panties fallen almost to her ankles.

"You want to know how you make me feel now? Sick! You make me sick!" he said, noticing that Rina showed no signs of moving.

He put on his shoes and laced them. Then he turned around and said:

"I've had enough of a good time. Maybe, though . . ." He hesitated a moment. Then, when he'd already begun walking, he turned around again, and added: "Maybe there's still one thing missing. Just this one thing!" And trying to overcome all the self-hatred that had been growing minute by minute in his conscience, he spat at her.

Several Sundays now, like tonight, Antonio came home after one. At the entrance, while he was whispering with Binda and Riboldi (someone from Via Aldini, who had spent that evening with them, Morini, and two models, at a night club on Via Forze Armata), he had seen Luciano come back with Rescalli and the entire variety troupe. With a smile, he had greeted all of them and then crossed the courtyard. When the door was closed, and he was passing from the kitchen into his room, he realized immediately that Carlo hadn't yet managed to fall asleep. In fact, he was tossing to and fro in his bed as if he were hot or actually in a sweat.

"You oughtn't get yourself all worked up and sick over what happened today," he said, standing there barefooted, in his shorts.

"I'll get sick over whoever and whatever I please."

"Suit yourself," replied Antonio, walking on his heels toward the door and extending his hand toward the light switch. "Let everybody suit themselves," he added, before turning toward the bed and drawing back the covers.

"Precisely," Carlo commented.

At the touch of the cold sheet, Antonio shivered. Still, he had so many reasons to be happy. Now, thrashing his legs about to warm them up, he seemed to be breathing in again the humid joyous atmosphere of a little while ago, and that dizzyingly powerful perfume rising from Lucy's breasts and the flower supposed to be covering them. And then he heard again, one by one, the comments stirred up every time he came back to the table after dancing with her; and the glances following and trailing after him almost everywhere; and among them, those dampish, dark, terrible glances of the big shot and Binda. Slowly, thus, his eyes smiling beneath their lids, he began to lose consciousness and fall asleep.

He might have expected anything. He was ready to admit that life might play all kinds of tricks, but not this. He, fall in love? Oh, of course, sooner or later, he too was bound to fall in love. But fall in love with her? And was he sure it was really love?

Then just one more thing to complicate the situation was that the following Tuesday he saw her standing there waiting for him at the factory gate. And because then, in order not to give in the least bit to his feelings, he'd pretended not to see her, there she was again, same time, same place, the following Friday.

"But what are you doing here? Don't you also get out at this time?"

"I asked for permission."

"Well now, look here. It's better for you to put in your full time because losing it for me is really not worth the trouble. What's been has been. Okay?"

At the time Rina hadn't replied. Only a little later had she dared to say that it was impossible to speak there in front of all those people coming and going, and that if he didn't mind they might see each other that evening after dinner at the same place as last time.

"Oh, all right. If you really have something important to tell me, let's meet there, at nine."

But at nine, he hadn't gone. And he hadn't gone on purpose.

He had left the house, yes. But instead of going to his appointment he'd walked back and forth on Via Aldini, forcing himself to take pleasure in Rina's waiting, and how he was insulting her again by his behavior. So that when he saw her coming home toward ten o'clock, instead of hiding he remained standing in the middle of the street and greeted her with a raucous laugh. Rina hadn't dared open her mouth. Silently, she kept on walking. Once at the entrance, she entered the court-yard only to disappear a moment later in the staircase. It had been precisely her way of reacting that now gripped Carlo's heart more than ever.

In love. And in love with someone from the other side. He couldn't understand anything any more! Despite his habit of getting to the heart of things, now he neither understood nor wanted to give in. It will pass, he told himself, and repeated it as if it were the conclusion of a long chain of reasoning by which he was struggling to prove the impossibility, rather than the difficulty, of arriving at anything concrete. It will pass. Instead, it didn't pass in the least. The evening hours, between Friday and Saturday, had been endless torture. He had tossed back and forth in his bed like a poor beast being torn apart by a pack of hounds: a beast that didn't want to surrender, but that felt its strength dwindling away and knew it was growing weaker and weaker every instant. A blow at his heart and a blow at his conscience. What would they say at the Circle? How would his Party comrades take it? He, Carlo Villa, the fierce Saladin, as he had been jokingly nicknamed because of his inflexibility, his refusal to compromise, he, Carlo Villa, losing his head over a silly little dame from the Christian Democrats!

Thus, all his reasoning had come to nothing better than this: to violate himself, or, rather, that part of himself which he had been taught to consider and which he himself knew to be his weakest side, the one that almost always ended up by provoking the gravest disasters and the progressive softening of his character and his will. And to keep right on, cost what it may. Wasn't there a perfect example of such softening of character right in his own home? Antonio, yes. And hadn't he also been motivated at first by lofty, sincere ideals? Boxing, glory; ideals that in themselves didn't contradict in the least other loftier and more serious ideals. But then, as he got ahead, boxing and glory gained the ascendancy, and cast out of his heart and con-

98

science what should have been and remained the fundamental purpose of his life. And now here he was reduced to the point of no longer even knowing what that purpose was. Here he was cracking up like someone in his second childhood, succumbing to the enemy's luxuries, and doing everything to deny that purpose and those ideals, even to destroy them. And to think that he, Carlo, too, perhaps for a more serious reason than a pair of boxing gloves and a number of rounds, should find himself in the same straits . . .

In the silence of that night, while his brother continued sleeping, Carlo tossed and tossed in his bed, then he gripped between his teeth whatever part of the sheet he happened upon in the dark, and began chewing on it as if this might give him some strength and peace. Because one could control one's feelings, yes, one certainly could! Even if one had to bleed for it, even if one had to suffer, very well, then, we'll bleed, we'll suffer, not to mention time, which settles so many things all by itself. In short, it might not have been only her, Rina. In fact, why had he accosted her, why had they gone together? If he'd felt that he really couldn't do without it, okay, he might have kept on, but always and only in the same way. That is, seeing her, speaking to her, having fun with her, but only in order to pour out on her all the fury of his hard, frustrating, and wretched life. Seeing her, speaking with her, having fun with her, but only in order to insult and humiliate her still more. Bring her to the point, in short, where she would be incapable of understanding any reasoning at all: neither the reasoning of her priests and nuns, nor that of any decent folk, anywhere. "Tomorrow, for instance," he said to himself and repeated it during the hours of that night, "tomorrow, when I see her, because now I can no longer resist seeing her, well, tomorrow . . ."

At that point his mind began to conjure up gestures and actions which he was the first to find repugnant, but which, precisely for that reason, filled him with a strange sense of hope:

99

that in this way he would be able to degrade Rina to such a point that he would then feel disgust for her and nothing but disgust. A little whore, a little whore veiled over more or less with goodness. Now he understood her. Faced with that argument, they were like all the others. Worse, rather. Well, let them have the worst. The Oliva family would suffer as soon as they came to know about it? It would be painful to them? Fine. If up to now he had suffered, from now on let them suffer a little too.

50

"Morini, always Morini!" Liberata shouted as soon as Carlo had gone out. "Goddamn him," she muttered between her teeth.

"That's enough of your goddamning!" Antonio said, purposely picking up his sister's imprecation.

Liberata didn't answer.

"I can't figure you out!" Antonio said, very calmly. "If people get on my nerves, I try to talk about them as little as possible. All of you, however . . ."

"All of us, however . . ."

"That's what I said, all of you . . . Look here, just to stick to you, for example, it would seem that Morini . . ."

"Morini?"

"Fascinates you more than all other men put together."

"You're crazy!" Liberata expostulated. Then, all at once, as if belatedly provoked by her brother's remark: "And you just quit saying 'man' that way."

"Why, how should I say it? Tell me. How should I say it? I'm waiting for you to teach me."

Antonio, who had set everything in order, seemed to be waiting there in the kitchen on pins and needles. He was pacing around the table, stopping from time to time as if trying to catch some signal or sound that failed to manifest itself.

"Listen, don't you think that Carlo . . ." he said, after a long pause.

"Carlo what?" Liberata rejoined.

But Antonio had no time to respond, because just then his parents entered from the bedroom.

"We're leaving," the father said. Then, turning to Antonio: "And you, listen. If you go out, just try not to come back again like the other times, in the morning."

Antonio's reply was limited to a grunted "All right." Then, while the two older folks were leaving the kitchen on their way to the Party headquarters, he lit a cigarette.

"I meant, don't you think that Carlo . . ." Antonio began again.

Liberata failed to reply; but as she stared at her brother, she seemed to sway for an instant.

"I don't know," Antonio went on, "but for some time now, it seems to me, he's been avoiding opening his mouth at all around here. Even tonight at dinner when all of you dragged up that business of the fine . . ."

"He's got things on his mind."

"Still, far's I'm concerned, I tell you again, if you have to put it up, the fine, I can help you out with something."

"And what can you help us out with? The money you pick up in your boy friend's stable?"

"Precisely."

"To me, I mean me, taking it would turn my stomach."

"Well, go ahead and turn your stomach! Still, as I've said, whenever you make up your minds, provided, of course, it doesn't make you all too sick, the thirty is at your disposal."

"You talk about thirty thousand lire as if it was nothing. And to think there are people . . ."

"What people? Do you or don't you have to get the money

together? Do you or don't you have to pay the fine? Do you want to paint the walls or leave them as they are? So, what difference does it make to you whether the money's coming from the right or from the left?"

There was a brief silence in the kitchen.

"Your friends seem to be late tonight," Liberata remarked at last. "Could they possibly have forgotten?"

"Listen to me, Liberata," Antonio replied. "You go to the movies or wherever you're supposed to go with your hysterical friend from upstairs; I'll worry about locking up here."

Some mouthfuls of food, some coils of smoke rising and floating silently around the lamp. Then, from downstairs, came three hard precise hoots of a horn.

"There they are," Antonio said, brightening up. "I'm on my way. And tell Carlo that far's I'm concerned, I'm willing. At least, he won't have me on his conscience any more as a traitor. And if he stops, so will you."

51

"Oh, Carlo, darling Carlo . . ." Rina murmured. Carlo didn't reply. His eyes glaring and childish, he stood there as if nothing mattered to him any more.

"Carletto . . ."

"What is it? What do you want?"

"Carletto . . ."

"When will you finally understand that now I've got it out of my system, you don't mean a thing to me?"

At these words, Rina's eyes, sweetly and somewhat desperately, began exploring Carlo's body all over until they came to rest at the point where his torso separated from the rest of him.

"Now, I haven't the slightest idea what use you could be to

me. Because, I told you, that's how I am. I don't enjoy being with anybody more than once."

For a moment, Rina allowed her eyes to dwell once again upon the warm secret shadow of that spot, then she looked up at Carlo with excited candor:

"Do you want me to show you that it's not so?" she said and timidly reached her hand out toward that point.

"Stop it!" Carlo shouted. And while the girl clasped him around the waist: "See what you're capable of doing? Virtue! Purity! You're nothing but a prostitute!"

"And you?" Rina replied, determined not to loosen her clasp by a fraction of an inch. "Do you see or don't you see that you love me?"

"Oh, so being like this means love?"

"It means you don't dislike it at all. Oh, Carlo, if you only knew how happy I am! If you only knew how since last week everything seems so much more beautiful. I don't know, I feel like singing. . . ."

"Cut it out, you little whore! Cut it out!"

"And why should I cut it out, when it's so lovely being here, knowing I love you and knowing that you too . . ."

"What, me too?"

"Open your mouth, Carlo. Come on, laugh, really laugh once. . . ."

"Laugh? What's there to laugh about?"

"If I let myself do what I've done . . . Carlo . . . But why do you smell so sweet tonight? Did you put on brilliantine?"

Now Rina was leaning her head on Carlo Villa's throat and little by little she began kissing him around the ears and there where his hair ended in a kind of fuzz.

"Doesn't all this filthiness disgust you?"

"Carlo . . ."

"Oh, now I get it. We stick to our ideas more than you do."

"Will you tell me how I am turning against my ideas, if I kiss someone I love?"

"If you kiss! And the other things? All the other things you do and have done to you?" Carlo yelled, once more swept by fury. "And now some fresh air! Fresh air! I haven't been able to breathe because of you!"

In his effort to get up, Carlo shoved the girl away so forcefully that Rina slid to the ground.

"I'd really like to know who taught you all these tricks!"

Instead of answering, Rina stretched out her hand where she thought she would touch Carlo's leg. Unable to find it, she lifted her head and said:

"Carlo? Come here a minute, Carlo. Only a minute, then I'll let you go. . . ."

"To do what? What are you kidding yourself about? Haven't I already told you I've no wish to make love with you tonight?"

"Carlo . . ." the girl murmured. Then, more strongly: "Don't talk like that, Carlo. You should know that things are not like that at all."

"No? Why? Perhaps you'd like to lay your hands on me again just to show me that I want to?"

"Carlo . . ."

"Because even if I did want to, I wouldn't do it anyway, understand? Not tonight, or ever."

"Carlo!" Rina cried. "Carlo!" she repeated. Then, overcome with sobbing, she fell back on the grass.

For a long while, Carlo looked at the girl who seemed like a heap of rags sprawled out on the meadow. But as he looked, the glimmering whiteness of her legs and arms set him trembling.

"Get up, now . . ." he finally said.

There was a new silence. Once again Carlo repeated his order. Now his heart was beating wildly and his conscience tearing him apart between the most contradictory ideas, the most contradictory decisions.

"Get up . . ." he said after a while, approaching Rina as if to help her rise.

104

As soon as she felt Carlo's body near her, Rina thrust herself into his arms, murmuring:

"Carlo, say that's not so, say that's not true. . . ."

Right then, Carlo wanted to clasp Rina to himself, take her head in his hands, press endless kisses upon her lips. Instead, he felt himself gripped by a contradiction that he himself couldn't comprehend.

"Carlo, without you . . . without you, I can't live any longer. Carlo! I can't! We must love each other. Perhaps that's why we came into the world. . . . Because what have ideas got to do with it? What have families got to do with it? Compared to this?"

"Well, you'd better get that out of your head! Even if the others wanted it, I wouldn't, I'd say No!"

"But why?" Rina murmured, looking at Carlo with streaming eyes. "Don't you really like to any more?" And since Carlo showed no signs of responding: "Then why did you do what you did?"

"I already told you the other time: to get it out of my system, to dirty you, and that's all!"

"That's not true, Carlo!" Rina replied, burying her head on his chest and beginning to sob again. "That's not true!"

"Yes, it is! And it's useless of you to refuse to believe it."

"But you're not the way you talk, Carlo," Rina exclaimed. "You're a good person. I've always thought so. And even if you came from hell, I'd love you all the same, I'd go to hell together with you."

Feeling Carlo's arms around her body becoming less rigid, she added:

"Because I know that being with you means being in heaven. . . ."

It was only a moment. Then, not knowing just how to refuse Rina's scent and her sobs of lamentation, joy, desperation, and fear, Carlo let his face draw close to hers. When he felt his lips about to touch Rina's tender, sweet, tear-and-saliva-washed lips, he pressed against her. But before he felt himself melting away entirely in her embrace, he had a momentary outburst of rebellion.

"Now that's enough!" he cried. "Now, go away. Go away for good!"

52

She would say nothing at home as long as everything remained uncertain. Then and only then would she speak. She was concerned about how her family would receive the news. However, this troubled her less than the possibility of presenting it as a decision taken with serenity: an honest, fair, normal decision.

What had happened that night had flooded her heart with a great strange faith. Great because, considering how that evening started and how it ended, one could only conclude that their love had made a step forward.

Strange, because she could not help thinking about all the difficulties the realization of their love was bound to run into. As far as Carlo was concerned, she was certain in the very depths of her heart. Now everything about him seemed to come clear: his contradictions, his attempts to break off, his rebellions, his wanting to insult her, his fear, anger, shame. Everything, absolutely everything. But she also understood equally well that he loved her, and the more he said No, the more he felt in himself the desire to say Yes. Furthermore, he had permitted certain expressions to slip out that evening that could have no other significance: "But do you realize where we're heading, Rina? Do you realize what could happen if one day we find out we're in love?"

And what greater, lovelier, holier thing could happen? So altogether certain of it was she that she was prepared to turn against everyone and everything to realize that love, as he insisted was bound to happen. And what is more, she was convinced that by so doing she would not be betraying her beliefs, not even by a shadow. Just as he would not be betraying his. "Basically," Rina said over and over to herself, "if ideas are true, and if someone believes in them, where else does their truth come from if not from life itself?"

53

Evening was about to descend upon the houses of the outskirts, and toward the west, clouds were piling up one upon the other like animals longing to embrace, melt into each other, and die.

The sunset shone through kitchen and bedroom windows, crept everywhere, reflected on floors, beds, tables, and clothes closets.

"Songs! Always songs! That's today's prayer!" old Oliva grumbled when a phonograph began playing with a noise like scrap iron up in the Meroni apartment. "What's the world coming to, with this kind of young people?"

But was it truly and exclusively the youth who were like that? For example, what right had the Schieppatis to complain even though they did nothing but complain all day long? That their oldest son had become a delinquent when they'd done everything possible to deprive him of whatever conscience he'd come into the world with? "You did it yourselves! You wanted it that way!"—that's what they ought to have been told, instead of wiping away their tears and consoling them. "You, with all your freedom and your glorious future! The Church and the Cross, that's what's needed, not the hammer and sickle! The Church and the Cross!"

Outside, the sky seemed unable to find peace. Purplish shadows, lightning flashes, ominous gleams. And a pinkish light spreading everywhere. Perhaps for this reason old Oliva felt more agitated than usual. Nor did the arrival of his son and grandson suffice to calm him. Especially since they had to leave, as soon as they came in, for one of their usual meetings. And all the more so because that evening Rina also wouldn't be home until about eight o'clock. Without all four of them around him, what was he but a king without a kingdom?

"But do you really believe, Enrica, that it's something important?" the grandfather asked his daughter-in-law, who was bustling about the kitchen.

"What do you think, Papa?"

"Nothing," the old man grumbled. "Nothing."

54

She felt exhausted. The leaden weight of that evening falling on her head; the hours and hours of work; the lie she once again had to tell her family; Carlo late; her doubts; the need to speak everything out and the need to be silent; and beyond all that, her desire, her desire that grew more omnivorous the more it was satisfied; and her fear that the world, being as it was, would make her lose everything at one blow: Carlo, happiness, and love. A fear that had become so great these last few days as to destroy whatever calm she still possessed.

Yes, now her mind was made up. Tonight she would ask him to assume responsibilities and to make promises to her which alone would enable her to speak out openly in her family. From then on, let happen what may.

She stood still beside the hedge, her eyes fixed upon the waters of the quarry, where the flames and shadows of the sunset were reflected in reverse as if sunk to the bottom of hell.

Even the sand and gravel path seemed inflamed in a reddish light, before succumbing entirely to the shadows. Just beyond the factories, the Bosiva chimneys and gas tanks, the trains from the North Station were passing and repassing, swiftly, indifferently.

"I was scared . . ." Rina said, when Carlo, pushing his bike, stood before her. Although Carlo had come to the appointment determined to be firm, as soon as he saw Rina's eyes glistening with her anxiety at waiting and her joy at his arrival, once again he felt himself lost. As usual, he could think of no other reaction than to be tough and violent.

"Do I have to get myself mixed up with somebody who's scared to stay here five minutes by herself?"

"That's not why I was scared, Carlo."

"Well, what are you scared of?"

For an instant Rina didn't reply, then she said:

"It's difficult to explain, Carlo. . . ."

"Why do you keep saying Carlo?" the Villa boy shouted.

"Carlo?" murmured Rina, with her eyes more than with her voice.

Carlo left his bicycle against the hedge, lit a cigarette, then he too began to gaze at the sunset reflected in the water.

"Don't let's spoil the few minutes we're able to see each other by arguing like this and quarreling," Rina said.

"Far's I'm concerned, this can be the last time, if you like."

A pause, during which a train clanged by full speed. Then from the Seveso line, another caught up with it.

"In fact," Carlo said, "if you really want to know, I don't ask for anything better. And don't think I'm just talking at random. That's not how I am."

"I know," Rina said.

"What do you know?"

"That you're not like that."

"Like what?"

"Talking at random."

109

Carlo felt himself weakening, although he had deluded himself into believing he had regained enough strength to speak with detachment.

"I hope you're not going to start that story all over again about being in love! Because I'm not in love with you. I may have a little crush, I don't deny it. But from that to talking about love . . ."

Rina remained motionless, her eyes gazing beyond the water. Carlo, who stood behind her, saw only her back.

"Besides, I think it will be better for you, too. Too many things stand between us. You know that."

And as the boy went on speaking he felt his heart breaking. He was lying, he knew. But why was he lying? To stick to a plan he had determined on? And what was a plan in comparison with this girl, whom he was already beginning to love, to adore?

"If we leave each other now, just . . ."

Carlo stopped as if it were difficult for him to breathe. He had flipped his cigarette far off and kept his hands buried in his overalls. "Maybe then it'll be possible to keep a nice memory of these few times we've seen each other. . . ."

Motionless, silently, Rina listened. It was when she started sobbing, and her entire back began to quiver, that Carlo finally understood. He grasped her arm and drew her close, saying:

"But Rina, you're crying. . . ."

"Carlo!" said Rina, bursting into loud sobs on his shoulder. "Carlo! How often must I tell you that I can't live without you any longer? Don't you realize that even those on our side might think of killing ourselves?"

"Rina! What are you saying? Rina—"

"I've been thinking about it for days and days. In the factory, at home, along the street . . ."

"Stop saying that, Rina! Stop even thinking about it!"

"You're right, Carlo. Forgive me. You're right. Sometimes I am so wicked . . ."

110

"Wicked? Why wicked?"

"Because I can't seem to convince myself that life means suffering. But suffering without you wouldn't even be suffering. I don't know, Carlo . . . All I ask you is not to leave me here, alone. I can't live like this, now. I'm weak, I know. But I can't, Carlo. I can't."

Carlo held Rina close in his arms and showered numberless kisses and caresses, now on her cheeks, now on her brow, now in her hair, in an effort to soothe her.

"If you only knew how long I've loved you! But first . . . First it was different. First, waiting didn't frighten me. Now it does. Now I know too well what it is like. Now I can't. It's annoying, I know. A girl like me shouldn't cry. But is it my fault if I love you? Is it my fault if my father, my mother, all my family are like they are?"

"It's not a question of fault, Rina. It's simply that the way things are, it's not possible."

"And why shouldn't it be possible? What harm are we doing? If it's true that you love me . . ."

Carlo made no reply to these words.

"Carlo, I've asked you something . . ." Rina said.

Once again Carlo failed to answer. He was desperately trying to restrain his hands, which longed to clasp Rina's body even more tightly than before, to contain her completely.

"Carlo, why don't you answer me? Why are you standing there like that? Why?"

Now Rina had lifted her head and was seeking amidst her sobs to look into Carlo's eyes. Exasperated by his incapacity to make a decision and follow through, Carlo now had dropped his hands.

"Why have you stopped holding me close? Carlo? Answer me. You are a man. I know. I've always known. And I'm in love with you because of that too. And because of that I'm willing to try to understand what you believe in. But now why

111

are you standing there like that? Don't kill me, Carlo. Speak. Say something! Anything, just a word. . . ."

For an instant Carlo looked at Rina. Then, his heart about to burst, he tried to speak.

"It means that both of us must realize, Rina . . ."

"Realize what?"

"That it's not possible."

A long pause.

"Unless you . . ." Carlo added.

"Unless I?"

"Unless you are willing to stay with me, live together, and that's all."

"No, Carlo, that, no. You shouldn't even ask it of me, because you don't really believe it yourself. You would be the first not to believe it."

"I wouldn't believe it? Then why have I asked you?"

"No, you just said it. But Carlo, the true Carlo, the Carlo I love, the Carlo I want to marry, that Carlo has a sense of honor. And it doesn't matter to me one bit that someone on the side that my family calls the side of the devil has a sense of honor. Honor is honor. And I want you to know that if I went with you it's just because of that. Because you have a sense of honor, Carlo. And to me honor is everything. The rest . . ."

"The rest?"

As if only now did she realize the serious import of everything the word contained, Rina did not reply.

"You see?" Carlo added. "The rest is so full of things that you can't even imagine. First of all, your family will say No. And then why do you want to go against them? Would you like to marry me and never see them again?"

Carlo waited a moment.

"Between them and me, who do you choose?"

"You," Rina said, looking at Carlo with sweet desperate firmness.

"Even now?"

112

"Now and for always."

"And your beliefs? Are you willing to give those up too?"

"If there's no other way out, yes."

"But then . . ."

"Then what?"

"Nothing, Rina. I've kept on asking you questions. Instead you ought to be asking some questions of me. . . ."

A brief silence. Then, speaking with decision and yet as if instead of speaking she were thinking aloud, Rina said:

"The right to try. At least that much will be left me. . . . They'll want to throw me out? All right, let them. But still I must tell them somehow or other. I've always told them everything. Why should I keep quiet now?"

Rina stopped a moment. She looked around. With amazement, she saw that the sky showed signs of calming down: there were still some clouds but now they seemed swallowed up in the slow immense spreading of the night.

"What I have to know before talking with my family," she said, "is that you're sure, really sure."

"Sure of what, Rina?"

"Of marrying me."

"Marrying you, how?"

"The how we'll see about after, Carlo."

Carlo hesitated a moment, then he said:

"It's just that, that I was trying to tell you. Marry you! Marry you! Those're just words, Rina! For example, I . . . in church . . ."

"I didn't say in church. I only said marry me."

Faced with Rina's clarity and determination, Carlo felt a sense of shame and inferiority. Undecided whether that had to do with the fact that she was a woman, or with the sweet limitless goodness that she continued to show, he made an effort to remain as calm and gentle as possible.

"Look, Rina, as I said before, coming here, I . . . But why do I speak like that? Why?" he cried, unable to bridle the force

113

of his feelings. "Why, when I do nothing but think about you, dream about you, see you everywhere?" Once more he had drawn close to Rina and taken her in his arms. "I know, I know that I shouldn't be in love with you. I know that I shouldn't talk of marrying you, not even let that idea enter my head. . . . But I love you, Rina. I love you. From that evening on, I . . . I don't know . . . Rina? Look, Rina? Oh, that face! Those eyes! You're not beautiful, you're not anything. Yet as soon as I see you, as soon as I think about you . . . Rina, my little Rinetta! Now do you realize that I'm also weak? Me, the ferocious Saracen! A pushover like the others. In fact, worse. But that's just why I can't. That's just why I mustn't. I have my convictions. I have my principles. And I'm not ready to throw away my convictions and my principles. I said that I can't, and I mustn't!" he shouted when he became aware that Rina showed no signs of saying anything. "Now, go away. If you really love me, go away! Because if I were to marry you, I might even boast of having managed to steal someone right out of the hands of those murderers who are your bosses and your priests! You understand? Now, go away! Go!"

But since Rina continued kissing him and, having pulled open the zipper, was pressing her lips against his chest:

"I said, go away, you little fool!" he cried, pushing the girl off. "Because if you don't go on your own hook, I'll chase you away!"

Rina refused to yield. With the same sweetness and strength with which she had been embracing and kissing him up to now, she turned toward him and pressed her lips again to the same spot:

"Carlo . . ." she began murmuring. "If you knew how many times I've dreamt of breathing close to your skin, as close as now. If you only knew how many times I've thought of being able to scrub your clothes, your jerseys, everything, even this dirty thing here, all covered with grease and rust."

"No. You're not scrubbing anything. All I can do, if you

really want to, is sleep with you. Because you please me. I can't deny that. You please me. . . ."

"That I please you isn't enough. Besides, it's not even true. . . ."

"It's true, Rina! Don't fool yourself! Three or four months of love like this, and then everything will be finished."

"No, it won't be finished at all. It'll just be more wonderful. Because when two people love each other as we do, there's nothing that can stop it."

"Not even your Church and your priests?"

"Not even those."

There was a pause. Then Rina said: "And now, Carlo, what more do you want?"

"This," Carlo replied, making her slide to the ground.

"But this is not more. . . ."

"What is it, then?"

"I don't know. Maybe it's the same thing. I only know that when I'm with you, I am happy, so happy. . . ."

"Then, are you willing to be with me even without marrying me?"

"I'm willing to do anything. But if you want me to stop thinking about it . . ."

"Rina . . ." murmured Carlo, kissing the girl's throat and nipping it. "That, no, Rina. No! Forget it!"

"Let me at least try, Carlo. Then if my family throws me out . . ."

"But I don't give a hoot for your family. Just don't think about that any more. Understand? Forget it."

"That also depends on you, Carlo. . . ."

"I know, Rina, I know. . . ."

55

Now the shadows had conquered even the last twilight glimmerings and, gliding down from the sky, had taken possession, deeply and secretively, everywhere.

Carlo took the bicycle, which he had leaned against the hedge. Then, according to their promise to take leave of each other where no one could see them, he approached Rina.

"So long," he said. "See you tomorrow. Here. Same time."

"Tomorrow. Same time." Tomorrow was the decisive day: the day of promises and pledges.

Needing to say no more, the faces of the two young people drew close to each other once again. A long kiss. Then another.

Over the grass, the breeze had begun to rustle lightly and set everything trembling, as if it were being born there in the bushes and fields instead of coming from on high.

56

Banging the silverware, blinking her eyes, and taking a gulp of wine without really wanting it, Liberata was waiting impatiently for her father and mother to make up their minds whether the television program was worth seeing or not. But they still hadn't made up their minds. And so, unable to stand it any longer, she rose from the table and noisily gathering up the dishes began shouting:

"When will you get it into your heads that I've got to speak to him? Once and for all, can't you get out from under our feet and leave us alone!"

"Who has to get out from under your feet?" the father replied.

Liberata didn't answer. Her mother, who had been aware for days of her daughter's growing edginess, looked at her husband as if pleading with him to be understanding and keep quiet.

"All right," Signor Villa replied. "If you say it's so good . . ."

"Not only me. Everybody's saying it," Liberata replied.

"We'll go then. We'll go."

Thus, the girl found the rest of the meal easier to swallow. She was so upset that she gulped everything down without smelling or tasting it. However, when, preceded by Antonio, her father and mother had gone out, and she finally found herself facing her brother, all her strength seemed to give out.

Carlo waited a few minutes, then took courage and decided to begin.

"Well, what've you got to tell me?"

"Carlo," Liberata said, "let's talk frankly. Up to now, you and I have been the only ones around here who've always said what they were thinking. . . ."

"I wouldn't expect it any other way."

"Okay, then, answer me. Do you really feel you've got a clear conscience?" Having spoken these words, Liberata lifted her eyes, which had been staring down at the floor following the movements of her broom and mop. But realizing that the speech she'd prepared that morning was fading away, she did not go on but remained perplexed for an instant.

"What are you driving at?" Carlo said.

For a moment, Liberata stared at Carlo, then grabbed the mop and, squeezing it out, mumbled:

"If you don't understand, then it's not worth while going on. It's enough that . . ."

"Enough that what?"

"Enough that you're not pretending."

There was a long silence in the kitchen. The broom struck

117

hard angry blows against the table legs, the chairs, the dish closet. Wet and soggy, the mop slid back and forth on the floor, leaving large shining swaths.

"Are you perhaps talking about Rina?" Carlo asked, turning a page of the newspaper he was reading.

As if struck by a whip, Liberata stopped at once. And at once she glared at her brother. But she said neither Yes nor No.

For a brief moment Carlo managed to face that glance. Then he tried to avoid it, turning the same page as before back in the opposite direction.

"You're not telling me that you're going out with that bitch . . ." Liberata said.

"Liberata!"

"If you think so much of her, you can also defend her! But as far as being a bitch goes, that's what she is and that's what she'll always be!"

At these words, Carlo felt utterly lost. If his sister's reaction was like that, what would his Party comrades say?

"Obviously our family is destined to trample on everything, even the most sacred . . ."

"But I'm not trampling on anything!"

"No, of course it's nothing!"

"And if you want to know, I started going out with Rina only to get my revenge for everything they had done to us. Except that then . . ."

"Then what?"

Carlo didn't answer. Silently he bowed his head and remained there, mute, defenseless.

"There are so many things you must realize . . ." he said after a while, gathering all his forces and beginning to speak again.

"It's enough to realize one thing! And that is, that what we stand for is more important than anything else, and that our convictions are not for sale!"

"But I haven't sold out our convictions. I believe in them. I believe in them the same as before, even more."

"Yes! You kid yourself you believe in them!"

"No. I'm not kidding myself. And besides, what gives you the notion that I haven't also thought about the difficulties of this kind of a relationship?"

"What did you say?"

"I said this kind of a relationship."

"A relationship, yes! A relationship that I can break, if you can't bring yourself to do it!"

"But why break it, Liberata? Why, if she's prepared to do everything?"

"Everything?"

"Everything."

"And just what does this everything mean?"

Again Carlo lowered his head and again remained there, silent.

"Would you mind explaining to me just what it amounts to? Give up her family? Give up her beliefs? But you're the one who should give her up first, that little hypocrite! You!"

"Liberata . . ." Carlo said, lifting his head again and gazing at his sister with mingled feelings of fear, terror, anger, and entreaty. "If I tell you that for days and days I've tried to get her out of my head and haven't been able to? If I tell you I'm in love with her?"

"In love? In love with that servant of the bosses and priests? But do you realize what that means? And remember: as long as I'm here, she'll never set foot in our house!"

"And if I want her to?"

"There are the fields! And there are other houses. But here . . . here, no! Here you'll see me dead first before I'll let her come in! Dead!"

Liberata stooped, picked up the mop, and carrying mop and broom toward the corner:

"I knew it," she said. "I had a feeling Antonio wasn't enough. But is it possible? Is it possible that no one gives a thought about me? What will I be doing in this house, when I won't even have you any more?"

119

"But I have no intention of leaving either you, or the house, or anything, or anybody. She'll have all the troubles, Liberata, not me."

"No. You'll have them too. Don't fool yourself. And if you don't have the guts to get rid of her, I can."

"How?"

"Shaming her and spitting in her face in front of everybody."

"No, Liberata, not that. Not that, ever!"

"And why?"

"Because Rina . . ."

"Rina what? Come on. Is she clever? Good? Honest? Holy? What's she got? Have you also learned the language of traitors?"

"Liberata!" Carlo shouted, rising from his chair.

A new long silence followed upon that shout. Liberata finished tidying up. Then, dragging her body as if it were painful for her to move, she went over behind her brother's shoulder.

"The least you can do is tell me why you ever started up with her?"

Instead of answering, Carlo sat down again.

"Oh, you haven't even the courage to tell me that? Or perhaps I rate so little around here that I don't even deserve to be told?"

"Don't you remember what you told me at the Circle, the night of the party?"

"I?"

"You."

"What did I tell you? I said she could have been the spy . . ."

"Exactly."

"But what does that have to do with the rest?"

"Nothing, Liberata. Nothing. But that you should be the one to turn against me . . ."

"Oh, sure! According to you, I'm supposed just to watch the last balls left to me around here drift away from this house, and not say anything about it."

"Liberata!"

"I didn't make up that word for men. Your fine brother did, the one whose path you're following!"

"Liberata! Now, that's enough! Because no matter how hard I try, it's only nerves keep me going. . . ."

"Nerves! Nerves! Redenta is right! The world's going to rot because men aren't capable of acting like men any more!"

"Liberata!"

"If you were really a man, you'd just screw that little bitch, if you wanted to, screw her, and that's all!"

"I did. Except that . . ."

"Except what? Your heart? I seem to hear it! Your heart! Love! Blind heart and blind love! Ah, but all of you, today as always, you're all blind! From the top of your heads to your toenails!"

A pause, during which two motorcycles were heard racing down the street, as if they wanted to destroy everything in their path; and in reply, Redenta's voice screaming from the window: "Go kill yourselves!"

"There! You hear?" Liberata said excitedly. "And she's got plenty of good reasons for screaming like that. Plenty of good reasons, believe me!"

Another silence. Then the girl said:

"I'd like to think that at least you'll be decent enough to give up your Party job. At least, you'll be that decent. . . ."

"I'm not giving up anything. On the contrary, if I've undertaken ten jobs up to now, from now on I'll do a hundred."

"Why?"

"Because I have something that I didn't have before."

"And what you have now that you didn't have before would be that little whore?"

"Liberata!"

"Whore!" Liberata yelled, trying to accompany the word with a coarse insulting laugh. "Whore!" But all that issued from her mouth was a cry.

"Liberata . . ." Carlo said. "Now what's the matter with you, Liberata?"

Liberata, leaning against the back of a chair, seemed gripped by a convulsion.

"Liberata . . ."

"Get out of here! Get out! Go where you have to go! You're all the same! All false, all selfish, all faithless and heartless. . . ."

She wanted to add more, to lift her head and shout as if cursing the entire world: "And me? What about me? Where will I find love? Who will give me love?"

Instead, with tremendous effort, she contained herself.

"Then, it's all decided. . . ."

"No. Nothing is decided."

"What are you waiting for?"

"Tomorrow."

"Why tomorrow?"

"Because I'm seeing her tomorrow, at the quarry."

Liberata's earlier aggressive outburst abated; but now her eyes opened wide as if she'd had a sudden vision of something she could take hold of to save herself: a mirror of dirty grayish water; and gravel all around. . . .

"I said get out!" she cried after a while, as if she were frightened at what was passing through her mind. "Go to your Rina! Go to the headquarters! Go wherever you have to, wherever you want to! Now at last I understand: in this life everybody has to use whatever weapons he's got."

"Liberata . . ." Carlo tried to say, drawing near his sister.

"Don't touch me! Don't touch me because it'll turn my stomach! And get out! Get out from under my feet, you too! All of you, get out!"

57

Money. The meals he ate sometimes in company with his
customers and sometimes alone: and then almost shamefully, as
if he feared everyone could read on his face the way he was
earning the wherewithal that permitted him to indulge in such
luxuries. The cinema. Clothes, not only those he wore but the
others he'd left at the boardinghouse. Fine, everything was fine.
But his home? His brothers? His sullen father, his anguished
mother? How many days hadn't he seen them? And then, the
self-disgust, a disgust perhaps only physical but no less revolting for that, for everything that those bastards made him do.
Untie this here; put your hand here. Or else, according to taste
and availability, you untie me, you put your hand here. And
those sighs and words he had to listen to? And then that afternoon he'd just got out of being kissed by that Swiss, the one
he'd never gone with before, but who was more or less known
to everybody in the Park and on the Via XX Settembre. Taking him in his car toward the Ticino River and then trying to
kiss him! "Look!" Sandrino had said, pulling away. At that
moment the sky through the windshield seemed soiled with
blood.

But how could he return now that his father, his mother and
brothers knew everything he was up to? And yet how he would
like to stretch out on the big couch in his own home! How he
would like to feel the warmth of flesh that didn't disgust him,
flesh amidst which he could laugh, innocently pinch, actually
relax and fall asleep! How he would savor again that odor made
up of dirt, soup, sweat, and urine emanating from the heap of
carcasses which his brothers had always made him think of
when, sprawled here and there, they slept like a litter of dogs.
Riccardo and Vittorio almost without breathing. Ninetto, instead, with such proliferating growths in his nose as to make

one think it was always stuffed. If only he could be sure he'd be received without comment. Instead, he was certain of the contrary. "Get out, you bastard!" they'd probably yell at him. "And don't ever dare show your face again!"

Tonight also he'd eaten, and eaten more than necessary. Each time he set his feet under a table, it was as if he wanted to rid himself of the memory of all the meals he'd eaten at home for years and years; and as if, besides, he wanted to regain his strength once more after that overwhelming weakness that had come over him in satisfying his customers' demands.

Ten o'clock. The city, the streets, the lights, the cars, the gardens, the trams—now everything seemed too big, too cruel. Something else, he needed something else. That big family of his, his own kitchen, his own bedroom . . . Not that room in the boardinghouse he'd been renting now for three weeks! Oh, of course, that room was more beautiful. But it seemed temporary, as if the walls were made of paper instead of bricks.

And yet even if he let himself be swept by these feelings, which little by little were making him heartsick, even if he decided to take a tram and go out there to Via Aldini, what would he gain by it?

Nothing, he knew. He'd never summon up enough courage to approach the house. Just like that Sunday when he'd stopped at the football field. But at least that Sunday he'd seen Vittorio. While now, it was so late . . . And yet! And yet, what?

58

Here it was. He mustn't remember that the last time he'd set foot in the house, he'd also stepped off the same tram after having done more or less the same thing.

And he mustn't remember that the only result of his seeing

his mother last time had been to make her weep and suffer. He mustn't remember anything. Step by step and he'd be there, with his cursed beloved Project to his right.

With lights at the windows and along the staircase. And perhaps at the Restellis' windowsill, Redenta. Because that gossip was always snooping, even at night!

For a few moments Sandrino remained rooted there. Then he set out toward the wooden fence dividing the large piazza from the highway.

Automobiles were passing rarely, but swiftly. And among one cluster or another of cars, there passed heavy trucks and trailer trucks, almost empty.

How different the buildings were from those at the center of town! It was a difference that only now he thought he understood. In fact, what he was seeing could not properly be called buildings. Even the newest ones that had been constructed up there near Novate, they couldn't be compared with those where his customers took him, or even with the building on Via Ausonio where his roominghouse was. . . . Roominghouse indeed! Roominghouse only in a manner of speaking. Because in view of its age, everything took place in silence and darkness. But after all, what else was there in his life that didn't take place in silence and darkness?

The only progress he'd made since he'd left home consisted in having learned how to defend himself and set the right price on himself. Granted it was disgusting, at least it was disgusting to the tune of thousand-lire notes!

Sandrino continued brooding and brooding; and yet little by little he felt himself growing deaf to and estranged from those places, that wooden fence on which years ago he'd clung so many times playing with his friends who could first guess the various makes of cars. Deaf to, estranged from those buildings, those streets. And who knows, maybe even from that life. Vittorio and Antonietta, who went to work, and once home, always found the same minestra, the same salami, the same carrots, the same chunk of cheese . . . Was that a life? The windows of his house, the table, the chairs, the kitchen, the big room, the couch, those poor bodies sprawled about . . . Wasn't it for them he was coming home? And now that they were within hand's reach, why not go on to meet them? Was it really and solely because he was afraid of what might happen? Or was it, instead, because he couldn't stand the thought of his heart breaking with homesickness and regrets?

His mother was right. And not only his mother, but also Redenta, the Villa family, the Meronis, the Balzinis, the Borgonuovos. They were right, all of them, all those who cursed the people with possessions and power. But since things were as they were, just calling meetings, putting up and tearing down posters, what were they gaining by it? The money stayed home on the other side? Fine. Then one had to go over to the other side. How? As he had gone.

It had been like a bright mirage that life had floated up before him. A mirage that became a golden, if stifling, cloak. And why not take it? Because of morality? What morality? They had clothes and he didn't. They had cars and he didn't even have a bike. They had houses, and he, here's what he had: that huge barracks over there spewing forth nothing but garbage and misery. . . . Go see it again, what for? To tell himself that one side was right and the other wrong? They shouldn't have let him realize that he possessed the means of enchanting and exploiting them. But since despite all their gold they were swine and sadists, swine and sadists and that's all, fine: he'd keep them there, on the leash, held by what they liked so much. And let them try to unhook themselves! Otherwise, if they wanted to do it gratis, let them go pick up other rich sadists like themselves!

59

He was the last to hop onto the trolley. A shiver, two. Then the tram moved off.

He bought his ticket. But instead of moving forward, he went to the back. Then he leaned against the handrail and began looking out.

Here was everything he knew so well. Here was everything he had left. Slowly, the moving tram and the dark silent night were destroying all of it: the lights, the houses, the bar at the right, the bar at the left, the one where he'd usually gone with Zebra, the little movie house, Rosa's door . . .

A stop. Then Via Eritrea, Quarto, the Purfina plant, the bridge . . . Good-by Vialba! Good-by Project, which for want of courage he hadn't even caught a glimpse of! But good-by until when? How long would he be able to resist? And stay away? And his mother? And his brothers? And Antonietta? How was it that now that he had come so close to them, had breathed the very air they breathed, he couldn't go on thinking of them as he had before? Why did all that squalor and poverty that he'd glimpsed again just for an instant, and that remained poverty and squalor even when decked out for a celebration, fill him with so dark and invincible a sense of dread? What the devil was he afraid of? Was he afraid that the squalor and poverty would grip him again in their monotonous inexorable vise, a vise that didn't hurt but little by little imprisoned and destroyed?

Slowly the tram sloped down from the bridge toward Via Espinasse. At the beginning of the street it stopped. A young couple stepped on. The ride resumed. Sandrino was still there, at the same spot, the breeze entering from the little window playing all about his shoulders and waist, as he stood there sucking his thumb, lost in his own thoughts and grief. At the next stop a woman climbed in. As the stranger paid for her ticket, she was choked by the scent of brilliantine coming from his hair.

"Smell that stuff all over him?" she said, turning to the conductor. "Now, why must young people today stink themselves up like that!"

Sandrino turned and glared at the woman as if to tell her that nowadays young people stank themselves up any way they could. Then he decided. Since the #6 tram passed the Park, he'd stop at the Park. And in order to destroy with one stroke his grief, his remorse, his homesickness, he would try to find another customer. One nail drives out another. It was late, but between Via Alemagna and XX Settembre they prowled around all night. Because, Madam, nowadays that's all that counts. That's all, he repeated, trying to feel sure of himself, and happy. And repeating it, his right hand felt in his trousers where he kept his wallet, swollen more with photographs than with money.

60

From that moment on, she'd had no more peace. The quarry, the water, the gravel . . . And now that they were there in front of her, she no longer knew what to think about. She only hoped Rina would arrive before Carlo. And so it was.

"Good evening," Rina said, as soon as she saw her.

Instead of answering, Liberata glared at her with so much hatred that Rina was constrained to lower her eyes. (Liberata would have liked to see her in her death agony at her feet. If she had to go up to her heaven, let her at least go watched by someone who cursed out her religion, her sacraments, and all her lying rot.)

"If you've come here for Carlo, you might as well go right back. Because you'll never see Carlo again. Never. Understand?"

And since Rina showed no signs of responding: "I said never again, and never again means neither now nor ever." Then unable to contain herself she hurled herself against the Oliva girl.

"Now call on him! Go on! Call on him, call on your Father in Heaven! Ask him to come and lend a hand to his Rina, who is so holy she even lets godless atheists take her out into the fields!"

"Liberata . . ." murmured Rina, trying to break away from the Villa girl's grip. "Liberata . . ."

"Don't call on me! Call on him!"

Liberata's eyes were fixed on Rina's. And the more Rina, terrified, trembled, the more Liberata's eyes lit up with joy.

"And Carlo? How did he, tell me, how did he embrace you? Like this? And when he was kissing? Answer."

"Liberata . . ."

"Liberata what? If I weren't afraid of ruining my life forever . . ."

In the struggle Liberata succeeded in knocking Rina to the ground, and now she was on top of her, choking her.

"I mean it. If it weren't for that . . . But now you understand what you've got to do?"

"Let me go, Liberata, let me go. I'm afraid I can't hold out! I'm afraid I'll scream. . . ."

"Well, scream! Go ahead, scream! What do you think, I'm afraid of other people? Things I think I've got to do, I do in front of everybody. Remember that night of the posters?"

"Stop, Liberata. For heaven's sake, stop. . . ."

"No, I won't stop. Because if it were up to me, what I did that night with your posters, I'd like to do now with your flesh and blood. I'd like to rip them to shreds. To shreds, whore!"

"Liberata . . ."

129

"Shut up! And if you're a woman, defend yourself!"

But in her terror and fear, Rina was unable to do or say a thing.

"What're you trying to prove, keeping quiet like that? That you're a saint? Who do you think you are? Say something! Come on! Speak up! Who do you think you are, an angel? Rina! I'm talking to you, Rina!"

"I don't think I'm anything. I'm just in love with your Carlo. Carlo is my life. And since you're his sister, I love you too. I'm not doing it to be an angel. I'm doing it to be happy."

"Happy! Happy on other people's misery! Is that what your charity amounts to?"

"But I didn't know this would make you suffer so much. . . ."

"Why, what makes you think I'm suffering now?" Liberata rejoined, as if she feared that Rina had understood or guessed something.

"I don't know . . . I only know that to come here and treat me like this you must be suffering, you must be unhappy. Otherwise you wouldn't do it."

"Sure. But if you really want to be just like your Madonna, you've only got to do one thing. Give up Carlo."

"No. That I won't do. I can't. Never."

"And I say you will! And right away!" Liberata shouted, again laying hands on the Oliva girl. "Carlo is ours! He's mine!"

There was a brief silence in which Rina, unable to collect her strength, seemed about to faint. Then, all at once, they heard both their names being called from the depths of the bushes. It was Carlo. Fearing what was about to happen, he had rushed out of the factory and pedaling like a madman raced to the spot. Not in time, however, to prevent Rina and his sister from meeting.

"Stop that!" he shouted, throwing his bike to the ground and running toward the hedge. "Liberata! Rina!"

Liberata let go of the Oliva girl and sprang to her feet.

130

"Liberata!" Carlo said, standing in front of his sister and staring at her.

Without rising, Rina murmured Carlo's name two or three times.

"Liberata, what have you done?" Carlo asked his sister. "Why?"

Liberata turned about. Then, as if she could no longer control herself, she burst into sobs.

"It's nothing, Carlo . . ." Rina said.

"What do you mean, nothing?" Liberata said amidst her tears. "Nothing? I was trying to kill you!"

"Don't believe her, Carlo. Liberata's just saying that . . ."

"No, I say it because it's the truth!"

"Liberata . . ." murmured Carlo.

"The truth! The truth!"

Then Rina, who had finally managed to get to her feet, drew close to Liberata Villa and, touching her gently on the shoulders, said: "But if it's the truth, Liberata, it's a truth that should be forgotten. . . ."

"Why?"

"Because we must go on living. Not only me and Carlo. You too."

"Go on living! Oh, of course!" Liberata cried, trying to regain courage. "Because for me this isn't the end of it, you can be sure!"

Then, facing her brother:

"You want to be her boy friend? You want to marry her? All right, go ahead. But first I'll do all I can to stop you. All I can. A bitch like her and a Communist like you will never work out together! I said never, Carlo, never!"

Carlo stood stock-still, unable to believe what he was seeing and hearing. He drew close to Rina and seeing how pale she was, how shocked, her hair all in disorder, her clothes ripped, he put his arms around her and murmured tenderly:

"Rina, my little Rinetta . . ."

131

"And you call her Rina! You call her Rinetta! Don't you realize that between you and her there are only priests and Masses and torn-up Party cards?"

"Liberata!" Carlo exclaimed, breaking away from Rina and menacingly turning on his sister.

"Let her be, Carlo. Tonight you must understand her. . . . Maybe Liberata has reasons that we know nothing about. . . ."

"You, perhaps. But he knows. But that's enough! I can do without your pity!"

"Why are you talking like that, Liberata?" Carlo said. "Why do you want to make a mess of things?"

"I'm not making a mess of anything! And you'll both find out when you come home. For you, I don't know. But for her everything will be finished."

Without another word, or turning around, Liberata walked along the hedge and, as if in the grip of a feeling stronger than herself, continued marching straight ahead.

61

Two or three improprieties were quite sufficient to summon men, women, and children to the windows of the Project, from which they looked down into the courtyard as Liberata was revealing with relish Rina's love affair to the Oliva family.

"What do you mean, it's not true? I've just left them rolling in the fields like a couple of dogs. Besides, you can ask Redenta. She was the first to tell me about it."

But at that moment Redenta wasn't present. Discovering that there was no meat in the house, she'd gone out to buy her usual slice of roast.

When she returned, the news of the scandal had already made the rounds, arousing the most disparate reactions and comments. Liberata had gone up to her apartment, but as soon as she saw Redenta she leaned out of the window and yelled:

"Is it true or isn't it true?"

"Is what true?"

"That Carlo's going around with Rina? Come on! Say it! Speak up! Tell those murderers down there. Tell them!"

The Oliva household was in a state of desperation. From his bed the mummy was pouring a steady stream of oaths and maledictions and, with whatever breath was left, shouting to be let out of bed to be the first to greet Rina when she came home. The others seemed torn between the effort not to believe and the shock of being overwhelmed by an event so degrading and so cruel. Silently they stared at each other as if they were experiencing the last moments of what was for them the only life possible. Then, when they attempted to find pretexts and proofs of the girl's behavior, everything came horribly back: the cinema she went to with excessive frequency, the Mother Superior who had reported that last Sunday evening she hadn't seen Rina at the oratory, and finally the lie about overtime work.

"I told you!" the grandfather cried. "But why didn't the good Lord let her die instead of casting her into this filth? Why?"

Commenting about it on the landing, Signora Meroni and Signora Balzani found themselves in agreement: "At any rate, that bunch up there won't be so stuck up from now on."

In the Cazzaniga and Riboldi households, however, there were those who maintained that they'd known about it all along, and others who simply refused to believe such a tremendous happening. Because if it were the truth, what would come of it? What other quarrels would they have to witness? And Rina? What would she do? Certainly the choice wouldn't be easy for her. And yet she'd have to make a choice. But which? The Villa boy or her family? The hammer and sickle or the priests?

The Olivas arrived at their decision by common agreement. Instead of waiting at home for Rina, they decided to go down into the street and slap her face in front of everyone. Aside from everything else, this demonstration of intransigence would serve as an example. The obvious result of such a scene would be the triumph of faith and honor. And it mattered very little that every curiosity-seeker in the Project would be looking down from the windows. So much the better. Once and for all, they would understand what it meant to have a faith and to be true to that faith to the limit.

62

As soon as Rina arrived at the Project, she knew that something was up. The windows were full of people, and her father and mother were standing in front of the kitchen gardens waiting.

"Where've you been?" her mother said, looking as if she wanted to burn her alive.

"Speak up!" the father snapped.

"This time at least there's no use lying."

For a few instants Rina was utterly bewildered. Then she said:

"Come upstairs. I'll tell you everything at home."

"At home?" the father said. "At home, you?"

"If you don't give up that antichrist," the mother explained, "you'll not set foot in our house again."

"But Papa . . . Mamma . . . please . . ." Rina murmured.

"Do you think we're ashamed because of all these people? We're defending your immortal soul and the principles of your religion! Why should we be ashamed? No, let them listen to everything, those atheists around here! Much better they hear it! Then they'll finally realize what kind of people we are!"

As Rina's father spoke these words, a long, low grumbling ran from window to window of the Project. However, as if the word had been passed along not to spoil the scene in any way by anticipatory remarks, no one retorted.

"Now then, what have you decided?"

"How can I decide if I haven't told you anything yet?"

"We know all we have to know," the mother said. "And not from you. Because you knew only too well how guilty and evil you were."

"But since that one up there . . ." the father continued, pointing to Liberata in the Villas' window, "since that one up there has spilled it all out here in front of everybody, you must proclaim in front of everybody that it isn't true!"

"What do you mean?" Liberata interrupted at this point. "What do you mean, it isn't true? It's absolutely true!"

"You shut up, you bitch out of hell!" Rina's mother screamed.

"I'll shut up when I'm dead."

At this point comments began rippling from window to window. But as if fearing that the passing minutes might favor his enemies, the father grabbed his daughter by the arm.

"Now then," he cried, shaking her, "are you going to get down on your knees or not? Are you going to confess here in front of everybody that you've made a mistake and from now on you'll have no more to do with that antichrist? On your knees! I said, on your knees!"

There was a moment of silence during which everyone remained still as if frozen, watching spellbound what was going on in front of the entrance. It was a moment that seemed an eternity; until, dragging himself with a supreme effort, the mummy appeared at the Oliva window:

"Answer, child of the devil!" he thundered in his cavernous voice.

At the shout everyone turned. Rina, her father, her mother, were just in time to see the old man, no longer able to hold himself erect, collapsing at the windowsill.

"Papa!" Oliva shouted. "Papa!"

"Oh God!"

"Papa!"

"Get going! Hurry! Hurry!"

Terrified at the thought of finding the old man dead, the two Olivas raced up the stairs, followed by Rina.

63

"No! Not you! You can't come in here any more!"

"But at least to see him! At least that . . ."

"Never again! Or if you really want to, confess your guilt in front of everybody and swear you won't see Carlo Villa again!"

The epilogue of the "scene" was being played out there on the staircase landing; Rina, having regained strength and courage, had made up her mind to face the argument squarely.

"Then you really don't want to keep what we have to say to each other among ourselves. You really want everybody to be in on it. . . ."

"Yes," replied the father. "Especially now that you've gone so far as to risk killing that poor old man."

"Go call Mamma, then."

"Mamma," her brother interrupted, "has to stay with Grandpa."

"Well, then, you take her place. . . ."

"No," her father shot back. "She stays where she is. Go on. Talk. There's not much to talk about anyway. You've only got to get down on your knees and beg forgiveness."

"If I've got to beg forgiveness for not having spoken about it earlier, I'll do it. But if I've got to swear not to see Carlo again, the answer is No. Not that. I'll never swear that."

"What did you say?" the father yelled, drawing close to his daughter.

"I said Carlo is mine and will remain mine."

"Rina! Do you know what you're saying?"

"Yes, Papa, I know."

"In that case, get out! Get out and don't ever show your face here again!"

Rina hesitated a moment. Then, trembling, she again requested permission to see her grandfather and her mother.

"What for?" her father replied. "You're no longer worthy of coming in here and touching us. Get out! Go wherever you like. But just remember, you'll never have a moment of peace again. Never again!"

Rina turned around. She felt like weeping but something within her told her to resist, to resist at any price.

She went down the first steps of the staircase amidst the silence of the few tenants who had had the courage to witness the scene. Then, when she was at the landing below, she felt herself reeling. She leaned against the railing, just in time to see Carlo through the fog beclouding her eyes. With choking cries, the boy was rushing up to her. As soon as he reached her he took her in his arms and, murmuring the tender endearments of someone very much in love, began embracing and kissing her.

"Damned atheist!" the father cried from upstairs.

"Satan!" the mother snapped.

"You want to rob us of our daughter, but you'll pay for it!"

64

They were strolling in the fields, between one hedge and another, like two poor desperate yet infinitely happy children. What would they do? And where would Rina go?

Questions to which neither of them knew the answers. Except to say: "I love you, Rina." "I love you, Carlo." And that was all.

From time to time Carlo told Rina that the courage she'd displayed that evening had made him love her more than ever and that she'd shown herself ready to be a real wife:

"I don't know, you seemed just like an angel. . . ."

"You're my angel, Carlo. And these are the wings protecting me." Rina touched Carlo's arms and as she pressed them she seemed to touch him through the cloth and grease stains and smell of his overalls down to the very marrow.

"Rina, now no one can harm us any longer. Not even Liberata."

"I know, Carlo. But if it were possible to be on peaceful terms with everybody . . ."

Instead, no matter where they turned, peace seemed out of the question. However, they had so much to think about that this seemed the lesser of their troubles. Meanwhile, night had fallen. Where would they go? Rejecting a hotel, rejecting the Villa apartment, not so much because of his sister's hatred as because it was better not to create further scenes, they finally decided to ask Redenta for shelter. Redenta would surely have room. But would she be willing to take on that burden, bring on herself the enmity of one group in the Project? And what about her brother?

For a while they continued their aimless wandering in the silence and darkness, one moment embracing, one moment gazing at each other, and calming each other's tears in a peace that was sadder than weeping. Until, weary, and realizing that in spite of all these happenings, tomorrow they'd have to go to work in the factory, since eat one must, they came to a decision.

Now the building was silent once more. Everything seemed as on any other night. They went over their final plans together. Still not altogether certain, Carlo said that he didn't know why, but he felt safe: deep down within, Redenta was on their side. It wasn't possible that everybody should wish them harm.

They entered the courtyard. They climbed the stairs. Although dejected, neither of the two felt either lost or defeated. When they came to the Restellis' door they stopped a moment. Then Carlo rang the bell.

65

Although the offer had been raised again, Luciano hadn't yielded this time either. The challenge G.P. had thrown him, the fervor and fury with which he pursued his ends, all this electrified rather than alarmed him.

In this skirmish between bidder and refuser, he didn't even know himself how much he was swayed by the chance of exploiting this relationship to the full, and how much by the tension aroused in him at the risk of such a violation: the last violation remaining for his body to submit to.

The number of ten-thousand-lire notes was raised each time, but each time he refused. And the more he refused, the more G.P. felt obliged, indeed compelled, to try to make him give in. And yet, deep within himself, Luciano felt that he wouldn't be able to hold out to the last. The seduction of money; the attraction of all the other promises; the role of the dark, inescapable demon he felt called upon to play in the presence of people like G.P. who had the means, the refinement and fascination of the strong, the rich, and the powerful—all these, like maggots, had gnawed away almost all his convictions. Only a few remained. But would those few suffice?

"If you agree, you know—and you don't know—what you can get out of it. . . ." And then, that struggle, with all its uncertainties and ambiguities, eventually filled him with tempta-

tion for an obscure, strange, but terrible attraction; an attraction
in which G.P.'s impressive physique didn't even play the major
part.

He climbed the stairs. As he passed Redenta's door, he heard
strange sounds; strange because usually at that hour Redenta's
apartment, like everybody else's, was silent and peaceful. But
lost in his own thoughts, he paid no attention, and went on.

66

"What do you mean, No!" Redenta cried. "If this is the famous
charity you're always preaching, you can change camps whenever you like."

She was at the window, shouting down at Rina's mother, who,
from the courtyard, had taunted her with running a roominghouse. And she was so furious that she gave the impression of
hurling the weight of her sorrows and shattered nerves on the
sanctimonious woman and the husband at her side, intending to
crush them.

"Because your Jesus Christ . . ."

"You keep your mouth shut about Jesus Christ! You're not
even worthy to mention his name!"

"I know that myself. But toward those who suffered, he . . ."

"Those who betrayed, that's what you should say. Because
Rina is a traitor," shouted Signora Oliva. "Don't talk to me
about suffering. . . ."

"And if I tell you she loves you?"

"Sure, you're just the one to know who loves and who
doesn't!"

"I. Yes. Because my Andrea . . ." and as if she were para-
lyzed by the image of that body dying amidst mud and snow,
she stopped.

"However, you better watch out. If you don't want trouble, you better not rent rooms."

"I'm not renting anything."

"I'll report it to the police."

"What police? The Egyptian?"

"And if you want my advice . . ." Signora Oliva continued.

"I don't need your advice nor anybody's."

"Too proud, eh?"

"Exactly! Since that's all that's left to me."

"What are you so proud about?"

"That I never betrayed anything or anybody!"

"As if everyone doesn't know you're keeping Rina only because of the rent she's paying. . . ."

"I'm keeping her because of your shitty face!"

At this point Rina's parents chose to break off the discussion, which had attracted the usual curiosity-seekers to the windows. Hastily they crossed the courtyard and went out into Via Aldini.

It was the truth. She had never betrayed anything or anybody, even though she was paying for all that blind stubborn loyalty with loneliness and shattered nerves. And what was more, for several days she had no longer had only one but two pieces of meat to pound and prepare: one for her brother and one for Rina. There they were: all she had to do was take a look out on the windowsill and there they were to the right. Now she had come so close that her elbow grazed against the paper in which the two cutlets were wrapped. Luckily, a bunch of parsley trembled alongside them. That at least was a green vegetable, and instead of rotting, the worst that could happen to it was to go dry. Besides, it was useless for her to have so many scruples. By now it was time to get to work.

She took the package and went to the table with it; opening it up was as if, instead of unwrapping the paper from that half pound of meat, she were unwrapping the entire uniform from Andrea's body. Yes, now she was going to have him right there, nude, with that wound ripping up his groin, that poor

141

groin which she'd never dared touch when it was alive. . . .
Then she took the board and meat pounder out of the pantry
and, compressing her lips, started pounding.

67

She realized that the first thing she had to do was to set her conscience at rest; and so she made up her mind. But she didn't
go to her parish church, where they would undoubtedly already
know about the situation. Instead she went to the church at
Bullona.

Entering, she trembled. When the priest arrived, she approached the confessional and knelt, and her heart began to
pound. She was hoping. She was hoping with all her soul, repeating to herself that she had need of grace as of the bread she
ate. The grace of feeling herself at peace with God.

Blushing, fearful, with pauses of silence, she recounted everything. And in the intervals of silence she waited with baited
breath trying to follow the signs coming from the grating: as if
the priest's breathing, his coughing, his movements might in-
dicate to her what he was thinking and what he would decide.
But although uttered cautiously, delicately, the answer was
explicit: No. No to her who had come there to confession
solely to hear Yes. Perhaps a Yes prompted only by pity, and
against every rule touching on her case. And instead: No. So
long as she had that kind of fiancé the priest could not give
her absolution. "It's too bad, I know, Signorina. Surely you understand that I'd like to help you. . . ."

She rose from the confessional, her soul shattered. She threw
herself down on a pew. She hid her face in her hands and began
to weep.

No. No to the wrong she had committed in sleeping with

142

Carlo before being his wife, and that was right. No to everything else, big and small. But why No to love? Why No to that which for her was the meaning of life? How could God possibly say No to a feeling that had been born when both she and Carlo were so small they couldn't possibly know or understand anything?

So then, although she knew that in her present state it was to no avail, she prayed and prayed intensely as if crying out to God that he at least could not, could not possibly fail to listen to her. She prayed begging forgiveness for what she had done. She prayed for Carlo. She prayed for Liberata. She also prayed for her family. Then she went out. But as soon as she was outside, what little assurance she had managed to gain, while she knelt on the bench, dissolved into nothing. No. And not only No for now. No for tomorrow. For the days after. No, for ever and ever. Either give up Carlo, or No. But why? Why must she find herself facing such a choice? Wasn't it enough that she'd had to forsake her family in order to follow her love? Wasn't it enough that she'd been thrown out of her home like a criminal? And now, also out of the church? Also out of the confessional?

As she walked along, Rina felt herself shrinking, becoming small, weak, without strength; oh, it was too much to bear, all those contradictions and that No at the same time. True, she felt a great Yes in her heart; and she had him, her Carlo, on whose shoulders she could lean and weep and cry out everything. But her peace of soul? And sleep? And the work during the day, the work she had to do well? And when very soon she would meet Carlo, what would they do? What would they say? And embracing after that No, wouldn't it be like embracing after her family's No? But if, kissing and embracing him, she felt only happiness, consolation, and a desire to kiss and embrace him all the more, how could she believe that that No was God's No?

143

68

"Carlo . . ." Rina said as soon as he stood before her. Then she lowered her head, as if she had something to conceal.

Carlo, who was waiting for her near the fence at the edge of the field, didn't let her finish. He clasped her to him, his eyes lighting up with joy.

"Oh, Carlo . . ."

"Later, Rina, later. Now just keep still and don't say a word."

"Carlo . . ."

"Look. Here is my mouth. Here are my lips. Here is my tongue. . . ."

"Carlo. . . ?"

"And here? Here is my nose. . . ."

"Carlo . . ."

Gradually, Carlo's head drew closer and closer to Rina's until their mouths joined in a long kiss.

All the weariness of a day's work, all the grief that had suddenly been revealed in his sister's heart, seemed to find compensation and peace in that kiss. They would never part from each other. Just time to catch one's breath and then start again. And again, closer, clinging all the more.

"Oh, Rina, my darling Rina!"

At such moments Rina understood and again asked herself how all this could be evil; and she would give herself entirely to the sweetness of those embraces and kisses, and no longer wonder about anything.

"I know that you're a bit down. Don't think I don't understand . . ." Carlo said, when he felt, rather than saw, a tear dropping between Rina's cheek and his. "A family's a family . . ." he added.

"Carlo? Don't leave me, Carlo. You're all that's left to me. Everything."

144

"Leave you? I'll never leave you. That's understood. Never. I'll follow you everywhere; if you step into fire, I'll follow you into fire."

"Carlo . . ."

"What is it, Rina? Tell me. . . ."

"I have got to thank you, Carlo. With all my heart. Do you want it? It's here. It's yours. Sometimes I wonder how they can possibly say you're a damned soul from hell. . . ."

Carlo smiled faintly, then continued embracing her.

"If you knew what I did today . . ." Rina said.

"Tell me. . . ."

A timid, almost shameful sob shook Rina's body.

"Come on, tell me. What did you do? You went to the factory?"

"Yes . . ."

"And you managed to eat something at noon?"

"Oh, as far as that's concerned, yes . . ."

"And now aren't you here with your demon?"

"Carlo!"

"Well, what more do you want?"

"Nothing. You're right, Carlo. Nothing."

"All it means is that besides being your husband I'll also be your father, your brother, your mother. . . ."

"Carlo? I don't know, there are times when I would like to die just to make you see how much I love you. . . ."

"Then why are you crying?"

"It's nothing, Carlo. . . ."

"Really nothing?"

Another brief pause. Then Rina said:

"This afternoon . . ."

"This afternoon?"

But how could she tell him? She was trembling. Yet Carlo was embracing her so tenderly that at last she decided to speak.

"This afternoon, when I left the factory I went to church. . . ."

"And?"

"I went to confession. I told everything. . . ."

"If you thought that was the right thing to do, you did the right thing."

After such a statement, Rina couldn't go on. She looked around. Then she gazed at Carlo and, trying to seem calm, she said:

"And do you think they gave me absolution?"

"Absolution, where?"

"In church. . . ."

"What? They kicked you out of there too?"

Rina didn't reply. She bowed her head and stayed motionless for a moment. Then sobbing softly to ease her heart, she leaned against Carlo and said:

"They actually want to force me to think it over. Everything . . ."

"Think over what?"

"Nothing, Carlo."

Another long pause.

Several bicycles, two or three motorcycles, and a group of workmen passed down the street.

"And now, Carlo, what should I do now? Tell me, Carlo. What should I do now?"

"Listen, Rina, listen carefully. . . . Rina? Are you sure in your conscience that you haven't done anything wrong?"

"Perhaps I shouldn't have made love with you before being your wife. But that night I just couldn't help it. I was afraid of losing you."

"And as for the rest. . . ?"

"As for the rest, Carlo, I love you too much and it makes me too happy. . . ."

For a moment Carlo remained silent, lost in his thoughts. Then he said:

"I don't know, Rina. Besides, with Liberata I find myself in a similar situation. . . ."

146

"Why? She still won't speak to you?"

"That's it," Carlo replied. Now it was his turn to bow his head as if he wanted to conceal the fear and shame that mention of his sister had stirred up in him.

"And if you tried again?"

"I don't know, Rina. I think it's useless."

"But I can't go on like this. I must do something. . . ."

"Well, then, try, Rina. At least your health hasn't suffered from it. You've got too many worries already."

"Perhaps sooner or later I'll find some priest who understands. . . ."

"Even if you don't find him, as long as you're not upset . . ." Carlo said, kissing her.

Rina held back for a moment, then gave herself once more to Carlo's lips, returning his kiss with an even longer and more tender one.

69

And there it was. Now she was alone, burdened forever with that image of herself which her conscience set before her eyes. She had suspected and even understood something from the start. But now that she'd seen herself defending like a beast a good that she considered exclusively hers, she could no longer pretend.

And yet what else was left to her but giving in completely to that hatred? It was a hatred that destroyed her but was her only means of taking revenge for all the ills, the grievances, the injustices to which she'd had to submit, first of all, having been born as she was born, that is, ugly, and without anything that might attract anybody; and then living as she had lived, between home and factory, always among people as poor as, or even poorer than, herself.

But why had Redenta, whom she felt so similar to her, lent a hand to this relationship? Why had she agreed to take Rina Oliva in?

Faced with this reaction, she was forced to wonder whether this was the same woman who'd always cursed out everything and everyone; the same woman who, on the evening of the posters, hadn't hesitated a second to join her in spitting all over them.

And as if the loss of that alliance weren't enough, she had to put up with Carlo's self-control. He might have left her the chance of striking back, on that one subject, at any rate, make him suffer the qualms of conscience. Instead, no. Nothing. As if everyone were seeing in that love affair the victory of their ideals, even the Party leaders reported that Carlo was as decisive and uncompromising as before, but even more so, his words and actions now had a gentle firmness, a conviction that made him more persuasive than ever.

It was obvious from their reactions that even they believed in the preposterous lie that at one time or another, in the lives of all men and women, love was bound to enter. If only it really would enter into everybody's life! Instead, too many were shunted aside as if they were made of stone and had no hearts like everybody else. Then, inevitably, everything turned to rage, hatred, poison.

And Liberata felt so full of that rage, hatred, and poison that she was sick of just standing there, inactive, without completing her revenge. She felt like the poor in front of the rich, like one who has nothing in front of one who has millions. And if, for those people, riches and millions were like a coat of gold attracting them with its glitter, its dreams, its promises, for her the happiness she saw in others was the sum of all the thwarted desires and instincts that her heart had never been able to satisfy. All those husbands and wives! All those families! All those babies! And here she was, still living with her father, mother, and brothers. Close her eyes to it? Pretend it

148

didn't matter? And for what? As for men, Carlo was her last remaining pride. Then why give up? To save her brother's happiness? But what about her happiness? Didn't her happiness count for anything?

70

Signor and Signora Villa had been in bed for more than an hour and Liberata was still up, waiting. Certainly not for Antonio, who she hoped, rather, would return later than usual, but for Carlo. So when she heard the door slam, she rose from the table where she'd been sitting intent on her usual knitting, and ran to open.

"May I?" Redenta said.

"Ah, it's you . . ." said Liberata. "Come in. Come in."

Redenta took two or three steps, looking about, then said:

"No one else around?"

"Who should there be? The old folks are asleep, and Carlo's out. . . ."

"I know."

"How do you know?"

"Before leaving he came to say good night to Rina. . . ."

"Ah! Really in love, then! Really rotten in love!"

Redenta Restelli looked at her in amazement.

"And if you want to know how I feel about the whole thing . . ." Liberata said. But struck by that glance, she stopped for a moment.

"If you want to know how I feel . . ." she resumed. "What gets me especially is that you, knowing what it means to have nobody, should knock yourself out lending a hand to a relationship which, the sooner it breaks up, the happier I'll be."

"If that's how you feel about it, I should have stayed downstairs."

"Oh, as long as you're here, you might as well sit down," Liberata Villa replied. "Then we'll talk."

"Would you like some coffee?" Liberata added after a while.

"Thanks, I've already had mine."

"But aren't you one of those who can't close their eyes until one o'clock anyway? So, coffee or no coffee, what difference does it make?"

Liberata went to the gas range, took a coffeepot, filled it with water, and began to prepare the coffee. Meanwhile, Redenta picked up the knitting, turned it from side to side, and complimented her on it.

"It's the only thing I can do," Liberata replied, as she turned on the gas jet with an angry flick of her finger.

"But why do you talk like that, Liberata?"

"Why? You ask me that, you who up to a few days ago did nothing but curse!"

"You're right," Redenta Restelli said, taken up short. "Excuse me. You're right."

"Because if you've come here to tell me something, fine; but if you've come here to preach to me . . . Especially when everybody knows that not an hour passes when you don't find some way of cursing out wars, governments, leaders, Church, love, and finally your Andrea. . . ."

As if she wanted to show how convinced she was of what she was saying, Liberata turned her head from the coffeepot toward Redenta. Then her eyes fell upon the brooch that held a faded, worn image of the deceased.

"You must have been in love with that one there, weren't you?"

"Liberata . . ."

"Well, just remember that I haven't even had that much in my life."

In order not to wake up the old folks and get them to come

out, Liberata spoke *sotto voce*. But the more her words seemed choked in her throat, the darker and more desperate they became.

"And that my Carlo should wind up in the hands of a disgusting Christian Democrat like her! I would have preferred a prostitute! A thief, I would have preferred!"

"Maybe you're just saying that because you don't know her. If you only knew how nicely she speaks of you . . ."

"And I hate her for that too."

"But, Liberata . . ."

"Oh, what are you trying to do now? Tug on my heartstrings?" Liberata replied as she watched the water boil. "I'd prefer to think she never says anything about me, I mean about me personally. . . ."

"She only says she'd like to see you content, and that she'd give anything to make it possible."

"Well, let her begin by giving me back my brother."

Liberata Villa lifted the coffeepot off the tile, went to the closet, took two little cups and saucers, two teaspoons, the sugar bowl, and put everything on the table. There was a long silence, broken by occasional faint sounds creating deep, almost rumbling, echoes in the room.

"How many would you like?"

"Two."

The sugar dropped into the coffee. The silence continued. Then Liberata said:

"Well, what did you come up here for?"

"What's the point of saying it, Liberata? It's only too clear that you don't agree."

"Agree? Agree about what? You make me laugh! Look here, I might have expected anything from you, anything except that you would take her part! I thought you were tougher, more like me. . . ."

"And if I told you that since that day, for the first time I

151

happen to feel something else besides a desire to curse, to send to the devil!"

"From that day, when . . ." Liberata demanded, once more glancing at the brooch.

"Why do you ask? You know. . . ."

"And you're doing all this in the hope that someday your sweet adopted child will remember you and treat you like her aunt, if not like her mother?"

"If that's how it turns out, I'll be very happy."

"Well then, get it out of your head! Once they're settled, one way or another, they'll drop you with a thud and good-by to what's been. At least that's how I'm treated by my brother."

"But what did you expect? Did you think your brother would never fall in love?"

Liberata failed to reply. Glaring at Redenta as if demented, she felt a momentary surge of physical, almost animal, fear. It was as if she were standing at the edge of an abyss. Then she said:

"I wasn't expecting anything. Besides, what have I got to do with all this business? What? Tell me!"

"I wanted to ask you if you knew . . ."

"Knew what?"

"Tonight Rina didn't stop crying for a minute. . . ."

"Sure, because everybody else in this jail around here is singing and dancing."

"I asked her what was the matter, but she only answered that she's happy. Then she went on crying."

"Okay by me. At least, now you'll understand that you're dealing with a cry-baby. These little saints are used to kneeling and praying and crying, and that's all. Besides, no one forced her to make love with Carlo. In your time, were you or weren't you aware of the possible consequences of your feelings for Andrea? Well then, Rina can put up with the same thing. And if she has any difficulties about it, you're there to teach her. You've had more than enough experience along those lines."

152

Just then someone could be heard coming up the stairs, then the screaking of a key turning in the lock. The two women turned around. The door opened. Carlo entered. He said good evening. Then, as if realizing that the atmosphere was anything but joyous, he asked what was the matter.

"She came up to tell me that your Rina has been crying all evening. . . ."

"That's not exactly how I said it . . ." interrupted Redenta.

"No, of course not!"

"She cried all evening," said Carlo. "And now?" he added.

"Now maybe she's calmed down. . . ."

"You see?" said Liberata, turning again to Redenta but pointing at her brother. "He's turned pale! Perhaps he's trembling. . . ."

"Can I go down a minute?" asked Carlo, trying to ignore his sister's remarks. Liberata rose from the table, took the cups, went to the sink, and turned on the faucet.

"If you wish," said Redenta. "Here's the key."

"And Gino?"

"Tonight he's staying at his seamstress'."

Liberata burst into a scornful laugh.

"A fine pair we are! Both of us with brothers in love!"

"Liberata . . ." Carlo said.

"Why not? Don't you see? That's all we needed to be even more like each other!"

Two, three squirts of water. Bangings of pots and pans as if, instead of simply two, one hundred cups of coffee had been drunk. Then Carlo said:

"Would you mind staying here a minute?"

Redenta nodded assent. Then Carlo Villa thanked her and went out.

71

He ran on tiptoe, noiselessly. In a darkness scarcely relieved by glimmerings of light seeping through the blinds, he saw the couch. He drew close and heard weeping.

"Rina?" he said.

Rina scarcely had time to turn around and there was Carlo next to her, close enough to embrace her. Her face was wet and the pillow and sheet were damp, too.

"Oh, Carlo! Carletto. . . !"

"Why are you crying, Rina? Why, if you know that I love you?"

Carlo had stretched out alongside the girl and was holding her tightly, caressing her, kissing her.

"Wait . . ." he said finally. "Wait till I take off my shoes. . . ." And without getting off the bed, managing with his toes, he kicked off his shoes. Then once more he was clinging to his love.

"I love you, Rina. You're everything to me. You are my wife, my star, my mistress. . . ."

"Carlo! Darling Carletto!"

"But now you must tell me why you're crying. Is it that business of the absolution again?"

Amidst her sobs Rina replied Yes, it was because of that:

"Carlo, if I go on like this, I'm afraid it will all come back to me again. . . ."

"What's going to come back?"

"If I tell you, maybe you won't love me any more. . . ."

"You can tell me anything, Rina."

"I'm back thinking again . . ."

"No," murmured Carlo. "Not that, Rina. Never. If you really love me, think about anything but that. Not that, Rina."

"But . . ."

"Rina, promise me you won't think about it any more. Promise me. . . ."

154

"Oh, Carlo . . ." said Rina, her arms tightening around Carlo's shoulders. "Oh, I do love you, Carlo!"

"Then why worry about the rest? And besides, it isn't true that everyone is unkind to us. . . . Look at Redenta. Before, she wouldn't have moved a finger for anybody, and now . . ."

"That's true, Carlo."

"Well then?"

"Help me, Carlo. I need you so much, now! Help me. I ask it of you as if I were asking you to kiss me. Help me. . . ."

"Of course, Rina, of course. . . ."

Little by little the two young people united into a single body on the couch, and Carlo's mouth was drying the tears falling from Rina's eyes, drop by drop: the sweetest, the most nourishing, the most precious sustenance of all.

72

He was her son, that was the sum and substance of it. And she was his mother. Did they understand what that meant? And for that reason and that reason alone she had swallowed all her pride, resentment, and scorn, and had gone to ask a favor of the Cornini family: would Luciano give her a name? Any name. Provided it would enable her to break into that bunch of delinquents and find her Sandrino again.

The reply had been to go to the Park between nine and ten, and on the avenue adjacent to North Station, or on top of the staircase giving onto the Via XX Settembre, look for a certain Darix; he'd surely know.

Without saying anything to anyone then, on Thursday evening, Signora Schieppati took her courage in both hands and once more climbed onto the #6 tram and got off at the Arch of Peace. But this time, partly because of her desperation, partly because of that name, she felt surer of herself. In fact, facing that abyss where women, automobiles, and motorcycles seemed to choke every other sound, she felt a sense of superiority, as if she were certain that tonight she would succeed in finding and taking her son out of that hellish snake pit.

She stepped forward on the avenue with determination. And with determination she began speaking to the first group of boys. But they didn't even answer. Either they knew nothing or they feigned to know nothing, all four of them remaining entrenched in the most absolute silence.

So she continued on, now and again lowering her head and lifting her hands to shield herself against the auto and motorcycle headlights, until she stopped before two boys speaking with a woman.

"Excuse me . . ." she said.

But the determination with which she stared at them made the three immediately realize that this had to do with nothing very pleasant.

"What? Do we know a certain Darix?" said one of the boys, after Signora Schieppati had spoken to him. "I think you must be mistaken. The only Darix I know is the one in the Circus."

"Same here," commented the second boy.

"And besides, who's this Luciano who's supposed to have sent you here?" continued the first.

"Then that scoundrel was telling me stories," murmured Signora Schieppati. "But why?"

"How should we know?"

"I'm only asking if you know Darix. . . ."

At that point the woman, thickly covered with make-up and doused with perfume, took Signora Schieppati by the arm, drew her aside, and said:

"Are you really his mother?"

"Whose?" replied Signora Schieppati.

"Darix's . . ."

"No. Darix's mother, no. I'm the mother of another boy. But only he can tell me where he is."

The woman looked her over from head to foot.

"Are you sure," she said, "that you won't make trouble? Not because I give a damn about these little worms here who are robbing us of trade. I only hope they go curl up somewhere on a hook. But I don't want any trouble with the cops. . . ."

"Neither do I. I only want to know where my Sandrino is. The rest is none of my business."

"Good, then go ahead. . . . You see that bridge there?"

Signora Schieppati lifted her eyes, but, nearsighted as she was, she could just make out on the other side of the foliage a flashing of more brilliant lights, and automobiles and motorcycles coming and going.

"There. Take that street and cross by the overpass. When you get to the other side, there'll be a stairway. . . . Ten minutes ago, he was there."

The information tallied with what Signora Cornini had told her. Signora Schieppati said thanks. Without looking again at the other two, who were being swallowed up in the darkness, she headed in the indicated direction.

At the other side she found not just one boy but a group of ten or twelve. They were whispering and laughing. From time to time they came close to each other as in a boxing match. In the darkness their eyes gleamed like knife blades. A burst of laughter. Obscene words. Voices imitating women's voices, or perhaps they were really identical. Some whistling. And as soon as one of the cars among the many passing showed signs of slowing down, four or five boys would break away from the others and rush over to the automobile, surrounding it as if by assault, like a swarm of starvelings.

Signora Schieppati thought: Who knows how many mothers don't even suspect their sons are here, selling themselves that

157

way. She felt her heart ache. But her grief was immediately superseded by an access of rebellion that lent her that last bit of courage she still lacked to confront the group.

"Excuse me, is there a certain Darix here?"

The boys turned around.

"What do you want him for?" one of them asked, getting up from the wayside stone against which he'd been leaning.

"I have to talk to him."

There was a rapid exchange of gleaming, greedy glances.

"You don't have to worry. It's a private matter, which concerns only me. Luciano sent me . . ."

At which, the same one who had got up from the wayside stone whistled.

"Darix!" he yelled. "There's a lady here looking for you. The 'boy' sent her. . . ."

"There he is. See him?" he added, turning to Schieppati. "Right there, at the end of the curve. . . ."

Signora Schieppati thanked him and went down the staircase. Here and there she met other boys. She continued toward the indicated spot.

"Looking for me?" the young man said, humming as he approached.

Signora Schieppati looked at him for a moment. Even in the shadow she could discern his dreadfully ingenuous face, the extraordinary beauty of which seemed ravaged and consumed by a secret evil.

"Yes, you."

"What for?"

"I need a favor."

"If I can . . ."

"It's about my son . . ."

"And who is your son?"

"A certain Sandrino."

"Sandrino?"

"Sandrino, yes."

158

"Sandrino . . . Sandrino . . . I think I know him. Wait . . . Is he from Vialba by any chance?"

"Yes," Schieppati said lowering her head as if she were overcome again, all of a sudden, by the fear and shame she'd felt the first time.

There was a silence. Then Darix said:

"And now that you know I know him, are you satisfied?"

"No. I want to see him."

"That's more difficult! You should have come a half hour ago. . . ."

"Why?"

"Well, Signora . . ."

"Tell me."

"He's found a friend . . ."

"So?"

". . . who invited him into his car. . . ."

"With a Como license plate?"

"No. Milano."

"And now you don't know where he is?"

"What a lot of questions!"

"But he'll come back here?"

"Depends. If he's made enough, he might go right back to his room."

"Where is he staying?"

"I don't know. Those are things each one keeps to himself."

"But that other one, you know him?"

"Naturally."

There was another silence. Signora Schieppati, who at first had felt very sure of herself, seemed to be falling back into disappointment and fear.

"Anyway, if you want to see him, all you've got to do is stay here and wait. As for me, just forget you saw me. Understand? Otherwise, your Sandrino'll also get into trouble. . . ."

For another moment the woman stood there, silent. Then she

said he needn't worry. She wouldn't make any trouble for him; not only that: she was grateful to him.

"Well, if you tell me to wait, I'll wait," she said. "But if he doesn't return, until what time can I find you here?"

"Depends. Maybe I'll have a call right away. Maybe within an hour. Maybe nothing'll happen. I'll stick around here till I get tired. . . ."

"But if I don't find him, when you meet him tomorrow, promise to tell him you saw me? And also tell him to come home. We won't do anything to him. Just as long as he comes home, neither I nor his father nor anyone will say a word about this."

"As far as telling him goes, Signora, I'll tell him. . . ."

"Thank you," Signora Schieppati said. "And you should also try to go home. Understand?"

"But I've never left home! I sleep in my own bed!" Darix exclaimed.

The woman looked at the boy, who was walking off, swinging, as if he wasn't in the least aware of what he was doing. Once more she began to be consumed with hatred. Hatred for the way the world was running, and for life as she knew it. Hatred for all those automobiles. Hatred for all that gold glitteringly displayed to those poor wretches, impelling them little by little to lose their conscience, their dignity, their honor, everything. And hatred also for those who were no longer capable of comprehending or holding their own. She, if she were asked, would starve first. She would eat dirt rather than demean herself making deals with those swine, and satisfying their demands. But she had been born and brought up in different times. And this is how the world was now.

160

73

She waited for two hours, but with no result. After a while, Darix returned and told her that tonight, at any rate, it was useless to expect him back. Then some character came down the staircase and the two of them went off together.

And now, here she was in her room about to go to bed, where her husband was sleeping poorly as usual, all sweated up with heat and wine. Would she have the courage to go back tomorrow? Or, instead, would she await the result of what Darix might tell Sandrino? But what result?

Undressing in fury, yet careful not to make any noise, she heard again what Darix said to her before leaving: "Don't worry about him, Signora. Your son knows how to defend himself. He manages to make money and keeps everybody happy. You'll see, sooner or later he'll find someone who'll set him up like a gentleman. . . ." Yes, a gentleman! But what kind of gentleman? Better, poverty. Better, hunger. Provided it was with a clean conscience, with dignity, with one's flesh and blood under control.

Now she had nothing. Not even the solace of tears. Only that wall of injustice, of vileness, and of corruption against which she could beat her head and break her heart.

74

Once again, after endless agonizing, she had made up her mind. Again, at the same time; but in another church, and more fearful than ever. The days passed; living that way two steps from her home like a stranger—worse, an enemy; the furious looks of her family whenever she ran into them on the stairs or in the courtyard; the greetings she no longer received from many of her companions, as if she were a traitor; and as for Carlo's relatives, Liberata's implacable hostility: all this had made it more necessary and indispensable than ever to feel at peace with God.

She entered the church, knowing everything she had to say and determined not to be blocked by the misgivings of any priest; no, she was resolved to battle.

Because she knew very well whom she would call upon for help at that moment: her Carlo. And so it was.

Firm on her knees, the veil covering her head, her elbows pressing against the ledge of the confessional, Rina refused to admit defeat.

"It's not possible," she said when the priest had confirmed his refusal. "It's not possible that the Lord shouldn't understand. . . ."

"That's what you say. But you know very well that there's only one way for you to be at peace again: give up that fiancé of yours. . . ."

"No. That I won't do. Never. . . ."

"Well, then, resign yourself."

"But why? Why, if I don't feel I'm doing anything wrong?"

"It's not up to you to judge whether something is or is not wrong. . . ."

Of course. She didn't feel as if she herself were making that judgment; rather, it was her conscience speaking. Yet the priest found ways of rebutting even this objection.

"Passion so often can twist the most honest conscience," he said. "Besides, you see very well that your family and parents . . ."

Her family, her parents . . . It was quite true. But family and parents were men and women and could be too closely attached to their own ideas. But he, the Lord . . .

162

"I cannot. It's useless for you to insist. If it's for a benediction, I bestow it willingly. But as for the rest, no, I would be failing in my duty. . . ."

She accepted the benediction like a state of grace. A state of grace that might keep off more terrifying thoughts. But until when?

She was afraid. Afraid of being unable to believe that a clean conscience was enough. Afraid that God might indeed demand that sacrifice. Afraid that Carlo might grow tired of her. Afraid, above all, that her incapacity to live in such a situation might drive her again toward the most desperate solution. But wasn't that a sin, the true sin against God? Wasn't evil really the rejection of love, and thereby of life? Why, if Carlo had promised to respect her faith. . . ?

"It always starts that way, Signorina . . ." (deep in her conscience she could hear the priest's voice again, like the mournful funereal echo of a bell) "but then, afterward, little by little, things change. Those are the tactics of the godless. They use them everywhere."

Tactics? Tactics, Carlo's promises? But why call them that? Why, if it was love?

"It may seem so now. But later, when youth is ended and love is also ended?"

Love? Love ended? But how, if she was sure that love, true love, lasted all one's life and beyond that? Because what was heaven, that heaven for which one suffered and strove, if it wasn't the endless continuation of love?

So. Once more down the steps and into the street. Once more amidst all those people, those cars, the trucks, the motorcycles, the bikes coming and going. The tram to take. The stops. Via Espinasse. The bridge. The Purfina plant. Via Mambretti. Largo Boccioni. And there against the hedge, Carlo waiting . . .

How could she go on living that way? Why had nothing come forth from the confessional but a push toward desperation and death? How could God's word be on the side of death? Her family didn't want her, not even the Church wanted her. . . . Only Carlo wanted her. And who was Carlo if not also one of God's children? But then why didn't God do anything to help her? Why would he want her to suffer so and weep so?

75

He hadn't said "you see" or "I told you so" or anything like that. He had clasped her close in one of those kisses that made both of them forget all life's grief, offenses, cruelties. Then they parted because that night they would be seeing each other again, to speak and comfort each other once more.

And in fact they met again a little after nine and began walking through the fields, the meadows, the byways. They walked without clearly knowing where they were going. At times they held each other's hands. At times they hid in some bushes, and kissed each other as if every kiss were the first or the last.

The gas flame from the Pero plant blazed ahead of them, and as soon as Rina saw it glimmering through the foliage she said it was their star.

So, amidst regrets, embraces, kisses, and entreaties; thinking of God, even when they clung to each other like two children filled with fear and love; seeing that God was not only not cursing them, but seemed to be smiling on them—Rina began to understand that to everything impelling her toward death, she must reply with life, a life still greater than her own or Carlo's, because, although coming from them, it was the life of another, of one who was not yet, but whom they could bring into being.

When she realized where her thoughts and desires were leading her, she felt pervaded by a joy greater than any she had yet known. Then she let herself go entirely in Carlo's arms, and as if she wanted to be heard by the entire world:

"Oh, Carlo, how beautiful!" she cried. "How beautiful!"

76

It was past five thirty. The whistles at Bovisa, Musocco, and Certosa had all sounded. But none of the workers had returned to the Project yet. The mummy was the first to notice it.

He was in bed oppressed by the heat, which made his breathing even more laborious, when he asked his daughter-in-law:

"What's that smell, Ernesta?"

"It must be the Pero plant. . . ."

"No. It's different."

"Then it must be the tannery they've put up at Baranzate."

"It seems to be coming from around here. . . ."

"Around here . . . What do you mean?"

"From the house. Open the window. Open it. I feel as if I'm suffocating."

Meanwhile, in the Balzani apartment, Elvira was shouting that she couldn't take it any longer.

"What are they trying to do? Turn us into a dunghill?"

"I've never smelled anything that stank quite like that," Remigio said. All sweaty and earth-stained, he had come upstairs for a chunk of bread.

"They're able to invent anything, things to go up to the moon with and things to go down to hell with," Redenta said with a final swipe of her iron, "but as for something to make life a little less miserable, no use asking them for that!" And she oughtn't be so aware that the stench was more or less like the stench of meat that's beginning to rot because of flies or heat. Since, when it came to rotting, everybody and everything was the same, those with souls and those without souls, beasts or humans.

"Can you hear me?" shouted Signora Consonni, appearing at the window and calling out to Signora Scotti.

"What is it? Are they spreading manure now?"

"I don't know. It seems to be coming from inside. . . ."

"Franco!" Signora Scotti shouted, turning to her son, who was playing in the vegetable gardens. "Do you get that smell down there too?"

"A little . . ." said Franco.

"Your nose is running!" the mother went on.

"I really think it's coming from inside . . ." Consonni commented.

"Yes, from inside," said Signora Borgonuovo, interrupting sharply. "That's what I say. From inside!"

Remigio was about to go downstairs with his chunk of bread and cheese when all at once he began looking around suspiciously:

"Mamma . . ." he exclaimed.

"What is it now?"

"Look here . . ."

"Well?"

"Don't you see that stain?"

Signora Balzani left her pile of laundry and bent down. About ten inches above the floor she saw a big stain spreading as if the wall at that spot was beginning to sweat. It was yellow, and touching it, her hands got wet.

"The smell must be coming from here. Smell it? It's the pipes!"

"What?"

"The toilet pipes!"

Signora Balzani left the kitchen and went to knock on the Borgonuovos' door.

"Vicenza?" she said and pushed open the door. "Vicenza?"

"What's the matter?"

"Come see. The pipes are broken!"

"The pipes?"

"The pipes! There's a big stain . . ."

"Where?"

"In the kitchen."

First Signora Borgonuovo, then Signora Scotti and Signora Villa, then, coming from the floor above, the Signore Consonni, Ruschetti, Rossi, and Vaghi, some alone, others followed by their children. All of them entered the Balzanis' kitchen to see what had happened. Drawn by the news, the children playing in the vegetable garden also came up.

"What is it?" Tino asked.

"It's that they treat us like animals!" his mother replied. She was just coming out of the Balzani apartment.

"Your mother's right," Signora Villa replied. "Like animals!"

"How many times have I told that antichrist of an administrator that it's necessary to check over everything. But they don't care. All they care about is collecting the rent. That's all! Nothing else!"

"And what's more, in advance!"

At this point, Redenta decided to leave her kitchen. She appeared on the landing.

"What's up?" she asked.

"Don't you smell that stench? It's like being in a latrine!"

"Where's it coming from?"

"From here," said Signora Balzani. "From my kitchen."

"What?"

"From my kitchen. The pipe's stopped up."

But that this theory was all wrong the women found out when they went down to the Rigutti apartment, where they saw, right over the pipes, although higher on the wall, a stain like that in the Balzanis', of which this was probably the continuation.

"Swine!" Redenta said. She had joined the other women in examining the stain. "Exploiters! I'd like to hear what excuses they'll find now, that gang up there!"

"Who? The Olivas? But they pray, and when you pray you're not even aware of smells!"

"And now? What do we do now?"

"Only one of our men is here! No. Everybody's at work. Except for that mummy, who only gets out of bed when he wants to curse!"

About twenty minutes later the men arrived. Faced with a barricade of wives, sisters, and mothers, they understood immediately that something extraordinary must have happened, and that perhaps the smell of which they'd become suspicious when they were approaching might be coming right from here.

"What's the trouble?" said Signor Balzani, the first to set foot in the courtyard.

"It's simply that our house is turning to shit!" replied his wife.

At this answer, all the women looked into each other's faces, as if only then did they suddenly realize how strong were the ties of their affection for these four poorly built and worse-kept walls.

"And they have the gall to call it a charitable and benevolent institution!" cried Redenta above the chorus of comments and protests. "Institution of hunger and poverty, that's what they ought to call it!" Then all at once as if she feared this incident might explode into thin air the meeting she had arranged precisely for that evening:

"And if that gang doesn't come down, it's just because they hate poor folks! As if their pockets were full of millions!"

"Right! At least on a thing like this they could be on our side . . ."

"What do you mean, be on our side," replied Redenta, "when to be on their own, they're capable of throwing their own children out of the house!"

And as Redenta looked up and saw that the mother had appeared at the Oliva window:

"I'm talking about you!" she yelled. "Understand? You and your whole sanctimonious family!"

168

77

They telephoned immediately to the offices of the charitable institution. But the administrator was on vacation and there was no one in the office at that hour who knew what to do.

Then the men went back to discussing the matter among themselves. Finally they decided to follow Carlo's advice: that is, to call a plumber at once.

"And who pays for it?" asked one of the men.

"First let's get this fixed," replied Carlo. "Then tomorrow we'll go to the offices of the institute and get matters straightened out with those crooks over there."

"But if they happen to raise a lot of questions?"

"What questions can they raise? We're entitled to this, and they're obliged to provide it. Do we pay them the rent? Yes? Well then, let them pay at least for the damages to their own walls!"

"Do you want to know how it's going to end up?" Signora Ruschetti remarked at this point, wishing to lend a lighter note to the proceedings. "They'll tell us that we eat too much, we're stopping up the pipes and making them burst! So the fault will be all ours!"

But this jest fell completely flat. In fact, everyone realized that the bitter irony might be too close to the truth.

The plumber came and inspected the pipes, followed, questioned, and advised now by this one, now by that. Until finally he said that at the moment, at any rate, there was nothing, absolutely nothing, to be done. It was necessary to break open the walls, clean out the pipes, and perhaps change them. Now that wasn't the kind of job that could be done right off the bat. Just breaking open the walls meant making the odor worse. Only one thing was certain: that nobody, at least on that side, should use any faucets or sinks or toilets.

"So now what are we supposed to do?" men, women, and children asked each other.

Open the windows: all of them. Sprinkle disinfectant on the floors; Lisoformio or something. And finally, since it was so hot, stay outside as much as possible.

78

Houses, people, walls, conscience, and lack of conscience. All one big rot! She'd made a fine attempt to thaw out her rage and her nervousness, showering Rina with as much care as she could, taking her into her house, treating her like a daughter! There was always someone, or when there wasn't there was always something bound to remind her again of the desperate conditions of her life and theirs.

All those people sweating. All those people swearing and cursing in the courtyard, on the staircases, in their rooms. Even the children had abandoned their games midway, as if they were in a daze. The only thing alive in the house was the Vaghis' phonograph blaring forth the strident voice of some night club singer. Redenta didn't know the name of the singer, but it was enough to hear her to know that on this subject, too, the world was on its way to the lunatic asylum.

79

"What did he tell me?" Signora Schieppati exclaimed. "He told me that tonight he's staying out. Since he's not used to living in cesspools any more . . . except when he goes looking in them for customers!"

A pause. Then the husband, busily fanning himself with the newspaper:

"Let's face it, he's absolutely right. Because this isn't an apartment house any more."

After her excursion to the Park, the night with Darix, Sandrino had returned. But he wanted everything clearly understood:

"Yes. I'm back. But as you told Darix, no discussions. . . ."

Thus, if only not to have Sandrino go off altogether, and at least be able to keep an eye on him, she and her husband had decided to accept that ultimate humiliation as well. The only point on which Signora Schieppati dared speak up was with regard to the brothers.

"Very well," she said. "But with the other six, I don't want any talk out of you. It'll be too bad, remember, if I find out that you've told them or even hinted how you go about making your money!"

"As for that, I believe they already know. And it's not my fault. . . ."

"That they already know is of no importance. What is important is that they don't also pick up your vice."

"Vice? What vice? Do you know what I like?"

"What?"

"Women! That's what I like! The rest is just for money."

And with an "All right. That's enough now," and a "Try not to give me a heartache," the discussion came to an end.

Despite everything, however, Signora Schieppati had not

stopped looking for work for her son. She'd scoured right and left. She'd involved everyone, even Carlo; and indeed Carlo at the moment was the only one who showed signs of really trying to do something about it. Ah yes! Seek and ye shall find, says the proverb. But up to now, at any rate, she hadn't been able to find a damned thing. Even this afternoon she had been to a cleaning and dyeing establishment on Via Donatello, where she'd been told they were looking for a delivery boy. Except that when she arrived, the delivery boy had already been found. Now, it no longer mattered to her that, faced with a concrete offer, Sandrino might turn it down. All she wanted was to have the job available, and throw it in his face. Let him know what his mother was doing for him and what she wanted him to do for her.

At the news that Sandrino wouldn't come back that night, Signor Schieppati remarked that he would also prefer to stay out in the open air, rather than sleep in that cesspool.

"Sure! So that you get crippled with rheumatism . . ." his wife replied.

Meanwhile, the children were complaining that they were hungry.

"Just wait a moment—everything will be ready in a minute."

80

They ate hurriedly, reluctantly, as if the stench had infected bread, wine, minestra, salad, and cheese. Few words were spoken.

And all the while, Carlo tried to conceal his concern over what might be the possible outcome of the talk with Luigi. Because although he felt sure of himself, he well understood the

172

importance it might have for Rina. Besides, there was the news he had to tell his family here in his own home where nobody knew anything: news that was burning his heart. But preventing him from bursting out with his happiness and pride, there was —his sister.

Hard, obstinate, violent, Liberata remained armored within her rage and rejection.

Day by day she grew thinner and her eyes sank into their sockets, as if she were being slowly consumed by a cancer. Not even her invectives launched against the charitable and benevolent institution, the administration, the rich, the priests, and the government seemed to give her the satisfaction she used to get from them.

Antonio, on the other hand, didn't seem in the least concerned about the incident of the plumbing. His indifference was such that Liberata, noticing the happiness rippling stealthily under his customary torpor, wished that something, at least some time or other, would go wrong with him too. Perhaps there was no other way of getting him back on the right track.

"It's really scandalous!" shouted Signor Villa as he bit into an apple and suddenly had the impression he was biting into decay.

"Of course!" Liberata shot back. "But since it's not enough just having to put up with traitors, we've got to invite them to our table . . ."

Stung by this new allusion, Antonio glanced at Carlo. Carlo replied with a steady determined look that stopped his reply in his throat. Then Liberata yelled:

"Oh, so now I'm not even worth answering? I'm talking to you, ex-revolutionary!"

Carlo gritted his teeth but didn't reply. There was another long silence. Then Antonio, trying to break the tension, made two or three jokes that fell flat. Only the mother laughed, and even she with moderation.

81

Night had fallen on the outskirts, clotting that first day of July in a sultry humidity. Houses, roofs, walls, streets, and asphalt were sweating forth a substance which, even in the dark, made them all seem to have grayish outlines.

And at the Project, in addition to the humidity, there was the stench which had become thicker and heavier with the hours.

"It's the rotten fruit of all the sins committed in this hell! That's what it is!" grumbled the grandfather, squeezing the rosary in his fingers. "And now, come on. Let's recite the Rosary. . . ."

In the Restelli kitchen, Carlo and Rina were waiting impatiently for Luigi's arrival. They were so wrought up and the talk with Rina's brother meant so much to them that they even forgot the stench engulfing the building.

"Well. Here he is. You stay calm. Let me do the talking. . . ."

Redenta went to open even before Luigi rang the bell.

"*Ciao,*" Rina said as soon as she saw her brother.

Luigi mumbled something, as if he were ashamed.

"Are Mamma and Papa well? And Grandpa?"

Instead of answering, Luigi looked at his sister as if he couldn't believe the innocence of her question.

"And the smell?" Rina said at last. "Is it just as strong up there too?"

Carlo stood close to her. By his stance, a bit ahead of her, he seemed to be saying clearly that henceforth Rina was his property and no one would be able to take her away.

"Well?" Luigi said, turning toward Redenta, as if he were in a hurry to get out of this embarrassingly painful situation. "You have something to tell me?"

"It would seem so," Redenta replied, indicating Rina with

her eyes. Rina's hands were gathered in her lap and seemed to be protecting something there.

"I said it would seem so," Redenta repeated, "because as you can see, here are two people who want to get married, and between these two there's his sister. . . ."

Luigi Oliva made no reply.

"Also, if I've asked you to come here, it's because I have more faith in you than in the others. And not only because you're young. . . ."

"Well?"

"What do you think should be done?"

"You are asking me?"

"And who should I ask?"

"We . . ."

"Never mind that 'we.' Speak up for yourself, say 'I.' "

"I should speak just for myself? . . ."

"But Luigi . . ." Rina said now. "Is it possible that you're that way too?"

"Because, if you come right down to it, just what has this poor girl done?" Redenta said. "Would you mind telling me? What's she done, that you treat her as if she were a devil?"

"You know what she's done. And there's no need to talk about it any further."

"Is that so? Even if I should tell you, for example, that your sister is expecting a baby?"

Luigi's eyes popped and he became pale.

"Now you're scared! Shouldn't you be telling me that children are God's blessings no matter where they come from?"

A long, strained pause followed these words. Rina had flung her arms around Carlo's neck, and he was caressing her shoulders, keeping his eyes on Luigi all the while.

"And someone's telling you this who wanted to have children, God knows, or whoever acts for him! Except that, in my case, your friends . . ."

175

"What friends?"

"Oh, those who were in charge before those who are now in charge. Yes, they! They killed the only one who might have given me a son, killed him before his time. . . . And now, look. You see him here, my Andrea? You see him? See, I'm embracing him, I'm kissing him. I embrace him and I kiss him in front of you and in front of everybody. I kiss him and kiss him! Because I loved him, loved him as no woman has ever loved any man. . . ."

A bitter hard sob racked Redenta's frame. Rina went over to her, drew her close, and said:

"Don't cry, Redenta. Don't cry."

"You see?" murmured Redenta trying to dry her tears with her handkerchief. "You see? This is not a girl, this is an angel. . . .

"And you?" she said after a while, making an effort to resume her normal tone. "I told you that your sister is expecting a baby and you stand there and gape without saying a word. What are you made of, you?"

Luigi Oliva seemed shattered by the news. But now he realized that he had to express himself in one way or another.

"What am I supposed to say?"

"What I made you come here for."

"And what's that?"

"To promise to talk with your family and try to bring them around. Because, listen. Maybe, before, you might have been able to kid yourself into believing they'd get tired of each other. But now with a baby on the way . . ."

"Bring them around, if I haven't even the courage to tell them?"

"But why?" Redenta exclaimed. "Is that so difficult?"

"If I come home with news like this my grandfather will never be able to take it. He'd never survive. . . ."

"What do you mean, your grandfather won't survive? He'll bury all of us!"

176

"And the other people?"

"What people?"

"People . . ."

"Oh, look here. To begin with, everybody in the Project would be pleased. . . ."

"Oh, these people here. They don't count."

"Counting or not counting, they're people like everybody else. And remember, you who talk so much about charity, just remember, if we can't agree on that, then those others . . ."

Redenta stopped for a moment.

"What others?" Luigi said.

"The others. You know very well who I'm talking about. The ones who are frigging everybody; frigging us from the front and then from the back!"

A shadow, almost as terrible as an omen, now passed over Redenta's soul, and her words seemed to loom up there in front of her eyes, not only in the shape of things, but also in flesh and blood. There was a long pause full of fear and bewilderment. Carlo had again drawn close to Rina, and realizing it was best to stay quiet, he was showing a firmness and calm much stronger than anger and indignation. Redenta, on the other hand, had begun squeezing Andrea's medal between her fingers, twisting it as if she wanted to tear it off.

"Well, do you promise to talk to them, and talk about it decently?" said Redenta, continuing to squeeze and twist the medal in her fingers. "I think now it's the only decent thing to do, never mind the beliefs on one side or the other."

Luigi hesitated a moment: a moment that seemed longer than a day. Suddenly gripped by a stronger feeling, he glanced two or three times at Rina, who glanced back as if trying to wring some sign of charity and help out of her brother.

"Talk about it? But how?"

"Listen," Redenta said. "If you, who eat the Host every day, don't know, then who does?"

82

Not a chance. Not only did he feel incapable of bringing them around, he felt incapable even of talking to them about it. Redenta had recourse to everything, even insults. She called as witnesses things she knew and things she'd scarcely heard about: Jesus Christ, the commandments, religion, the state, the Church, politics, war, peace. But Luigi said he simply wasn't up to bringing news of that sort home to his family. It was impossible. Telling them that would mean killing them.

Thus, loneliness had given Rina another terrible turn of its vise. Everyone from her side rejected her, that was true; but she had Carlo and now the baby. And Carlo and the baby were more important than everything and everyone. God must understand that; she was sure of it. And she was equally sure that in one way or another he would bend down and bless her.

By now it was eleven o'clock. Voices, comments, complaints continued rising from the courtyard. The stench showed no signs of abating. Some were swearing and some were blaspheming. Some were nauseous and some had headaches. One was saying he'd lose a night's sleep, and another was yelling that he was going to sleep out in the fields. One clamored to have all the directors of the Project hanged, and another proclaimed that the only thing to do was to stuff yourself with sleeping pills and knock yourself out.

After Luigi had left, and she had exchanged a few words with Rina and Carlo, Redenta went down into the courtyard; it was as if the negative result of the conversation had once more unleashed her rebellious instincts. From time to time her voice could be heard above all the others: Andrea, the Albanian front, the fascists, the priests, hunger, luxury, stinking water, latrines, the charitable and benevolent institution . . . Words. Shouts. Some applause. Some forced chuckles, just to keep going. And from time to time, as a background, the whistles of trains going to the North Station or climbing the Bovisa grade; the roar of a motorcycle; and from the little bar on Via Lessona the strident and absurd echo of rock-and-roll.

On the couch in the kitchen, Carlo and Rina forgot everything in their embrace. Little by little the words of endearment whispered into each other's ears, and the kisses they exchanged, undid all their sorrow. Because between kisses, they assured each other that they were happy, that they would try, in spite of all difficulties, to respect each other's ideas, and that they would love each other forever. And from time to time, Carlo's hand touched Rina's belly, and gently, timorously caressing it, he said:

"Here. Here . . . Here is my . . . your . . . our happiness. Here is everything, Rina. Oh, Rina, darling Rinetta . . ."

83

As if to prove that he wasn't going to leave him just because of that, G.P. had insisted on taking him home. With his complex of reverence toward the rich, he would never, but never, have consented had he known what had happened at the Project that afternoon. After all, he still had some dignity left.

As he stepped out of the car, his friend asked him whether he was content. Luciano said Yes.

"Then we'll see each other again tomorrow?"

"Sure, tomorrow."

With a roar the car leaped toward the end of the street, where it made a turn.

Now he felt weary, soiled; almost like a rag. It was as if a knife had entered his flesh and cut every fiber, revealed every secret. Now he had nothing more to defend, nothing to aim for. From now on, everything would be only a monotonous variation of things already done and known.

That what had happened to the pipes was what had happened, Luciano understood right away. But he had other things to worry about. Assuming that his body was still worth worrying about at all.

The lire notes had grown and grown; so had the insistence; so had the fascination and the sympathy that G.P. had been able to generate; at last he had given in. Now he no longer heard anything. He no longer heard the jiggers of whisky falling into the glass. Nor the rustling of the lire notes that G.P. had piled up on the night table like the last stake in a wager. Nor the voice that from time to time was saying: "And if this isn't enough . . ." He was only aware of a hidden bleeding, a sense of having been utterly violated, and that, henceforth, nothing could cure that wound and that outrage. Yet, at the same time, he also felt that what had happened had been fated.

It had been a question of days, months, years. But from the time when eight years ago he'd begun saying: "Yes, I'll meet you"—a Yes that certainly was nothing compared with the Yes he'd said tonight—his destiny had been sealed. So why complain?

He climbed the stairs with a kind of indifference. He, the handsome one; he, the "boy" of the Project; now he was no longer master of anything, not even of his own flesh. It was two o'clock. The stench notwithstanding, men, women, children had retired into their bedrooms. The windows were flung wide open like giant mouths from which issued breathing, and as people tossed in their beds, the screeching of springs, the rustling of blankets and even of sheets could be heard.

He opened the door. He went into the kitchen. His mother and sister were sleeping. They had been the first to use, and advise others to use, sleeping pills. He turned on the faucet.

180

He drank his usual ladleful of water. Then on tiptoe he crossed the women's bedroom.

As soon as he was in his room he flung himself onto the bed. Well, that was over with. Everything was settled.

But that he should have to end his day putting up with that stench! With the tip of his toe, he pushed against his heel. . . . A slight effort and the shoe dropped, with a dull heavy thud.

Redenta, whose room was under Luciano's and who had barely dozed off in a kind of sleep, woke up again. She realized at once where the noise came from and what it meant.

"That poor bastard!" she said. Then she turned in bed and, cursing everyone and everything, tried to fall asleep once more.